THE LIGHT IN THE BARN

A DOMESTIC THRILLER

SUSAN P. BAKER

REFUGIO PRESS

THE LIGHT IN THE BARN

Copyright © 2025 by Susan P. Baker

Produced in the United States of America.

For information and/or permission to use excerpts, contact:

susan@susanpbaker.com

 Formatted with Vellum

THE LIGHT IN THE BARN

DEDICATION

For my parents, Andrew Z. and Jean M. (Attwood) Baker. You're in my heart and thoughts every day.

IN MEMORY OF MYSTERY AUTHOR

BARBARA BURNETT SMITH
who encouraged me in the beginning.

PROLOGUE

A piercing cry in the middle of the night woke Aurora, who then lay peering at the ceiling in the dark. Did the shriek come from a dream? The cry echoed in her mind, but so often the sounds from dreams did. Now, the fullness in her middle, from the late-night drink she'd had before bed, urged her to use the restroom. She extended her hand to touch her new husband, Jeff, not wanting to awaken him but to reassure herself he was there.

Her hand made contact, not with Jeff's warm body as she had expected, but with the cold comforter covering his side of the bed. Disappointed, she rolled over to determine whether he slept on the edge or whether he really wasn't there. His side of the bed was vacant. Turning back, she pulled her little clock from the drawer in her bedside table. The illuminated dial read two a.m.

He'd called and said he'd arrive late. Though normally he'd stay in a motel, he wanted to be home for their yard sale the next day. She appreciated his phoning in the evenings to let her know his status. But still, sometimes she wished she'd married someone who wasn't in sales, someone who worked in town, a nine-to-five. She pushed away the memory of such hours on the part of her first husband,

1

who had evolved into an emotional abuser—dumping her—divorcing her—and marrying another woman. Jeff was different, and she loved him for it. She just didn't love the traveling salesman bit. And though he called when he would be home so late, she wondered whether something additional could be holding him up. Another woman, if truth be told. Her second husband could be engaging in the same activity as the first.

Wanting to quell her racing mind, Aurora pulled the covers up to her chin. She needed to get back to sleep. The yard sale would be a long, hot, intensive day.

During their whirlwind courtship, as one of her friends called it, Jeff had been attentive. He'd been in town a lot more than he was now. He'd called her frequently. They'd spent the majority of their waking hours together. Since Aurora had been married once before, she recognized when the "honeymoon" was over, but she'd hoped with Jeff romancing would last a little longer. Before they'd married, he made sure she realized his career in sales meant he'd be gone a lot. She understood. She really did. She didn't mean to feel the way she did, but you feel the way you feel, one of her friends said.

Aurora gave up and crawled out of bed to go to the restroom and get a drink of water. When she entered, a light flashed in her eyes. The light came through the window above the bathtub. She pulled back the shower curtain and looked out. There it was again, brighter now. The light came from the old barn—what she called a barn—an old outbuilding her grandfather had built years ago to house his stuff—his tools and all the detritus he'd collected during his business cleaning up building sites. The light flashed several more times. For goodness sake, the yard sale of the junk she'd inherited was the next morning. The idea someone wanted to burgle the barn the night before, when everything would be priced to practically give it away, was ridiculous.

After using the restroom, she returned to the bedroom and pulled her bathrobe over her nightgown. Slipping her feet into some clogs, she snatched her phone from the charger in the kitchen, unlocked the back door, and stepped out.

The scent of the gardenias she'd planted next to the outside steps greeted her. Stifling, humid night air engulfed her, making a robe for warmth unnecessary even though a proper garment to wear outside. Crickets chirped. Fall in Texas took longer and longer each year to arrive. The sliver of moon didn't shed enough light to see her way, so she aimed her phone's flashlight toward the ground. In setting up the yard sale, they'd left a path to the barn, so as not to trip over Grandfather's junk, which they'd laid out in several piles.

Aurora planned to yell at the intruder when she grew close and hoped they would leave without a confrontation. She suspected the culprits were kids, seeing what they could get away with. Every few moments, the light would flash again. Just one flash, maybe only one person.

When she was about twenty feet from the barn, she raised her light and waved it around the front of the building's windows. "Come out of there!" She stepped around a pile not far from the doorway. Noise like lumber clattering against lumber came from inside. Aurora approached the entrance. She grasped the edge and pointed her light in the direction where the last beam had been. The items she'd stacked up to take outside in the morning looked undisturbed. Waving the light around again, she expected to come across the person but didn't. Whoever it was could be hiding, or could have gone out the side door, though the rusty hinges would have squeaked.

Without warning, someone leaped out of the shadows and knocked Aurora to the ground. Her cell phone fell away. Adrenaline spiked through her body. "Hey," she yelled as she landed on her arm, momentarily stunned before rolling onto her stomach. Bits and pieces in the yard clattered as the person stumbled over them in his race to get away. He had been too fast for her to see his face in the dark, but she thought the silhouette was of a man. He was larger than her. When he rammed into her shoulder, she felt like she'd been tackled on the football field, not that she'd ever played football. He could have been a large teenager. He dodged some of the stacks of her grandfather's junk, as if he knew where they were located. When he hit the street, he ran up the slope toward town. The streetlight half a block up showed a person dressed in dark pants with a dark hoodie pulled over his head.

After lying on the ground for a few moments, recovering from the fright, Aurora found her cellphone and brushed herself off. Her shoulder ached as did the arm she fell on, but nothing felt broken. Wiping the dirt from her lips and chin on her sleeve, she walked back with shaky knees. She latched the back door and checked all the windows to be sure they were locked. They wouldn't keep out anyone who really wanted in, but she'd hear them, at least. After debating whether to call Jeff and find out when he'd be home, she thought not. He must be close at such a late—or early—hour. There was nothing he could do. The person was long gone and hopefully wouldn't return,

In only a few hours they—or at least she— needed to be up and ready to open their yard sale. She could tell Jeff about the burglary once he joined her outside. Now, she needed to get some sleep—if she could with her racing mind and wobbly knees.

Shedding her robe and clogs, Aurora settled back into bed, thankful she had peed before she'd gone outside. Shaking her head at her perverse sense of humor, she turned toward the wall and pulled the covers up under her chin. Shivering, she realized the outside air couldn't have caused a chill. She might be suffering from shock. Focusing on deep breathing, Aurora hoped she'd be able to sleep at least an hour or two, though it was unlikely.

CHAPTER
ONE

Aurora reached out again and this time her hand touched a warm body. Jeff had arrived home sometime in the past three hours. Careful not to awaken him, she slipped out from under the covers and picked up the clothing she'd set out the night before. Treading lightly, she went into the bathroom to change and get ready for the day.

Annoyingly, she almost tripped over Jeff's discarded clothes lying in a pile next to the tub. Would it be too much to drop his clothes into the hamper even if it was the middle of the night? Closing the door, she opened the hamper and picked up his clothes only to catch a sweet, cloying smell on his shirt. Holding it to her face, she was almost overpowered by the aroma. Her heart plummeted to her knees as she sank down onto the toilet and cupped her stomach in an effort not to cry. The first time she'd smelled a fragrance, not hers, on his clothing, she told herself he must have been in close contact with an employee on his route who had overdosed her body with perfume. The present scent was so strong, almost an odor, there had to have been close bodily contact. Jeff loved her, though. He was bound to have a rational explanation.

She dropped his clothes into the hamper before blowing her nose and knuckling her eyes with the tissue. She had stuff to do but couldn't help thinking about her situation. He couldn't be carrying on with other women. He'd married her such a short time ago. She dressed and washed her face and rubbed sunscreen on her cheeks and nose, so she wouldn't burn while she was outside at their barn sale. Her chest hurt when she looked at him, snoring softly like an innocent boy.

She wanted to approach his side of the bed and beat him with whatever was handy, a shoe maybe, yet she still wanted to give him the benefit of the doubt. He knew she was still recovering from the hurt she'd felt when she'd discovered her first husband had screwed around with her best friend. During their brief courtship when she'd told Jeff, he had sworn he'd be faithful forever.

Aurora hurried into the kitchen and put the coffee on. Leaning against the kitchen counter, waiting for the brew to be ready so she could pour herself a cup, she made a decision. She wouldn't think about her suspicions for the rest of the day. There wasn't time. She had to get out into the yard and finish setting up everything before people began to arrive. Her friends were coming to help, but there was more to do than they'd accomplish by opening time. Always more to do. She drew a deep breath. She'd have to think about her discovery later.

Once outside, Aurora set her coffee cup just inside the barn where she could snatch a swallow in-between tasks. One after the other, Aurora carried the wood-framed windows from the barn to the yard, the autumn breeze blowing powdery dust across her face, causing her to sneeze. Right off the bat, she'd made the mistake of licking her lips. She'd had to rinse her mouth and brush her tongue to get rid of the gritty particles. Her mouth still tasted like a whisk pan.

Now, the sun peeked above the flat horizon. The light revealed enough detail to the items they were selling that Aurora could turn off the old shop light hanging precariously from one of the less-rotted beams. The row of windows she and Jeff had stacked against the barn's front wall over the last few weeks didn't look like it had shrunk any, but glancing back into the yard, she knew better. She shook out her gardening gloves, brushed herself off again, and stomped the ground to shake loose debris from her work boots.

When she'd gone to the barn earlier, Aurora had done a brief inspection to see if she could pinpoint what the middle-of-the-night trespasser might have been after. Nothing appeared to have been moved. For several weeks they'd been going through the junk, tossing some into the back of their old work truck for disposal, and setting other bits aside for the sale. Even when Jeff wasn't home, Aurora spent a good deal of time sorting and dusting off the stuff. Her grandfather had been a great collector. She'd yet to see anything worth stealing, but everyone had different tastes.

After she'd stacked the next five windows, Aurora stopped to catch her breath. She pulled the ratty toweling from her shoulder and whacked the windows to remove loose dirt and paint chips. Lengths of dirty white rope hung from the wooden window jambs. She took a minute to brush cobwebs from her torn, faded black jeans and dust from her pink T-shirt. The sun had risen higher, allowing Aurora to better see what she'd accomplished. She'd have the first lot ready on time, though not without more perspiration running down her neck and back. Cars had yet to pull in front of their property, but soon people would be crawling under or tearing down the barrier she'd erected across the driveway.

"Hey, Aurora. I'm here." Sarah, her best friend from the sixth grade, announced herself. The two women couldn't have been more different physically. Sarah was tall, big-boned, with pale blue eyes and sandy brown hair. Aurora had hazel eyes. Her hair was dark brown, when she hadn't colored it a different hue. She didn't consider herself petite, but she didn't stand more than a smidgen over five-foot-three.

Sarah had parked somewhere out of sight, thoughtfully leaving space for estate sale buyers to pull in front. She jogged to where

Aurora waited at the entrance to the old barn. They air kissed each other's cheeks.

"So glad to see you." Having help would be a relief. "Remind me there's something I want to talk to you about later."

Sarah stepped back and peered into Aurora's face. "Something I did?"

"No. It's about Jeff." She sighed. "Later though, okay?"

Sarah's eyes scanned Aurora's face. "What do you want me to do?" She wore a tight, navy T-shirt, emblazoned with the icon for the blood donation center, and jeans. Her light brown hair was tied up in a ponytail, leaving dangling crystal earrings to catch the first rays of light along with her pale blue eyes. "Doing this all by yourself?"

"Jeff's still sleeping. He didn't get in until way early this morning. I'm not sure when, but after two." Sarah was smart enough to figure out his behavior might be the later topic of conversation.

"Uh huh," Sarah said and tucked her cell into her back pocket.

"Did you notice the signs I put up when you were driving over here?"

"Yep. Good locations." Sarah pulled gloves from her other back pocket and put them on. "Okay, I'm ready. Point out what you want me to do. Are you going to let people go inside the barn and look around? Or are they restricted to what's outside?"

"Mostly outside. They can go inside if they don't go past the area I roped off this morning. Otherwise, I think it would be a madhouse. Could you set up the folding table and the two chairs and place them in the best spot for Georgina to take people's money? I have to hurry and get more stuff out of the barn."

If she could drag out two windows at a time, she could accomplish a bit more before any buyers came, and she could start on the stack of doors. Those, she would only be able to manage one at a time. She wanted the stacks both inside and outside of the barn to be manageable for people to look at.

Sarah finished with the table and chairs and returned, scoping out the piles Aurora had made. "I know it seems like everybody in town renovated a house in the last few years, but this is ridiculous."

"Grandpa had his business for years. Almost until he passed away."

Sarah began carrying boxes and jars of what she considered trash into the yard—hinges, jars of nuts and bolts, doorknobs of various vintages. "Would somebody really want this smelly, greasy old junk?"

"Selling it will help with our own renovation costs." Aurora and Jeff planned to restore the old farmhouse to its original state as much as possible, maybe even add an additional room.

A car stopped in front. It was not opening time yet. Attending garage sales where the host had opened early and people were already poring over stuff by the time she got there had always annoyed Aurora. She didn't want to be one of those hosts. She was going to stand her ground and stick strictly with the advertised time.

Taylor arrived and joined them in the barn entrance, looking the contents over. She wore a lavender polo-style shirt under denim overalls. Her long tawny hair hung down her back in a braid. "Boy, y'all have a lot of junk."

"Good junk," Aurora said. "Salable junk. Would you help Sarah? Grab the next box—or take the crate over there into the yard."

A big woman, Taylor was heftier than Sarah, but she lifted weights and worked out regularly. She should be able to carry more. "Hey, Aurora, what about the stuff in the shed behind the crime scene tape—which, by the way, is cute—an original idea that only a mystery writer would think of."

"I don't know about that but thanks. The stuff taped off inside the barn hasn't been sorted yet." Aurora wasn't going to mention it may have been disturbed overnight. There was no reason her friends needed to know what had happened. They'd just fuss again and try to get her to install a security system. "The tape will help keep people out—I hope."

"Where's Jeff?" Taylor picked up a plastic milk crate full of assorted metal stuff. She set it down again and dragged it to the collection in the middle of the yard.

"Sleeping. He needs his rest," Sarah said. She and Taylor exchanged glances.

Aurora continued dragging wooden doors—some with screens, some without, some with bloated veneer chipping off, some mostly intact—past the tree where she had stacked the windows.

"Oh, yikes!" Sarah jumped back from a box.

Aurora ran to her. "You okay? What happened?"

"There's a skull ..."

"A rabbit's skull is all. Throw it in the box. Maybe someone will buy it."

Peering over Sarah's shoulder, Taylor said, "I'd forgotten your sense of humor, Aurora. I'm so glad you've moved back. We're going to have a lot of fun."

"Ugh. I'm not touching that thing," Sarah said. The skull, picked clean without even a small piece of fur clinging to it, lay close to the area of unsorted stuff. "Makes me wonder what else is buried back there."

"I didn't know you were so squeamish, Sarah," Aurora said. "I found a snake's skin yesterday. The skin was old, though, and crackled and fell to pieces when I picked it up." She grabbed the rabbit's skull and threw it into the box Sarah carried.

"Was it a rattlesnake?" Sarah asked. "You could probably do something with the rattle part."

"No, but I heard someone came across a nest of rattlesnakes in a field when they were clearing brush the other day."

"I take it you only asked friends to help you who aren't particularly put off by stories like that," Taylor said.

"I didn't realize Sarah would be," Aurora said to Sarah's back.

"I heard you. The skull surprised me, that's all. And I noticed on your schedule you have Georgina handling the money and not helping back here. I'm sure that's probably because she wouldn't want to risk breaking a nail."

"Yeah, right," Taylor said. "Not that it's easy to break a nail when it's dipped. What about those things stacked around the far side of the barn?" A bright blue tarp covered most of a pile of something. "Are we supposed to tackle that before the sale opens? There isn't much time."

"No. Jeff put it aside to possibly use for our own renovation once we go through and clear out this stuff."

People had begun to gather at the entrance on the far side of the tape. A man called out. "Come on. Open up!"

Aurora took Sarah's arm and said to both friends, "Georgina's jogging up and looks like she'll be ready as soon as she's made herself comfortable."

Georgina's keys hung on a strap around her neck. She had on thick, black rubber sandals, black leggings, and a long, striped tunic. Her toenails were painted a shiny green, as were her fingernails. She brushed off the seat of the folding chair and set her cell next to her elbow as she sat down. A small notepad and pencil lay next to a metal money box on the table in front of her.

"I don't see how as a cop she gets away with her nails always being so perfect," Sarah said.

Taylor said, "You know how persuasive she can be."

"No. I mean wouldn't she break a nail or something when chasing criminals?"

Aurora rolled her eyes. "We can ask her, if you want, but the dip stuff is made of plastic, I think."

"Sorry I'm late," Georgina said, when they reached her. "I just couldn't get out of the car without hearing what was coming over the radio. You won't believe what they were reporting." Her pale blue eyes were wide as she glanced from one of her friends to another. She whispered, "Another dead woman."

"Oh, gross," Sarah said. "Let's talk later."

"Yeah." Aurora's face scrunched up. Overhead, some wispy clouds wandered across the sky. The sun had completed its mission, brightening the landscape. "Right now, we've got to let those people in or face their wrath. Let's go ahead and open. I hate to do it early but ..." She could feel guilty about it later and nodded to Taylor.

Taylor snatched the tape off the nearest tree, crossing in front of the man who had called out, and announced: "The lady you need to talk money to, if you find something you want, is the one in the pink shirt and black jeans. The rest of us are just here to help. We can carry stuff if you need us to."

The complaining man shouldered past her, grunting.

Sarah said, "I hope Jeff is going to come and help carry the heavy stuff, Aurora. Surely, he's had enough beauty sleep by now."

Aurora glanced at the back door of the house before turning to greet the prospective buyers. "He really hasn't slept much."

She was a little annoyed, because he'd been the one to suggest they hold a series of sales. They had both known he'd be gone a lot, but he could have figured out a way to get home earlier if he'd really wanted to. Jeff was the one who'd wanted to buy Harold's share and move to the farmhouse. At least, that's what she remembered. In the days after the will was read, when they were discussing what she and her brother had inherited, didn't Jeff say he'd like to renovate the farmhouse? Harold sure didn't. Wasn't it Jeff? Sometimes their discussions left her confused.

Since she and Jeff had moved from Houston, Jeff's mood had fluctuated. Aurora wished he'd go back to being as charming as he'd been when they were dating. Now, Aurora noticed little things she hadn't been aware of before, a little put down here, or an insult there. When she called him on it, he always apologized. He claimed he didn't realize what he was doing. It must be a carryover from the kind of behavior he and his ex-wife had gotten into. Mostly he treated Aurora like that when he had long days at hospitals not far from their home. Fortunately, though, when he returned from his out-of-town trips, he was usually back to his sweet self, at least most of the time.

CHAPTER
TWO

Aurora and Sarah stood in the yard at the edge of what Aurora and Jeff called the driveway but was really a fifty-foot-wide graveled path that had never been paved. Eager people pushed in to find the good stuff. At least that's what they heard one woman say. Taylor and Georgina chatted with the diverse group of customers, greeting them and pointing to Aurora. Who knew remnants of demolition sites would be so popular? Apparently not Aurora's grandfather, or Amos might have hosted his own sales.

Aurora's brother, Harold, had commented over the years about how much their grandfather simply enjoyed spending his weekends on the hunt for what Harold and Aurora and their grandmother considered trash. There were jars of screws and jars of nails and jars of bolts and nuts. Tools, some antique, hung from the walls nearest the barn's entrance. Their grandfather had painted the wall yellow and outlined the tools in red—pretty artsy for a country boy who had gotten his GED in the army and never shown any interest in furthering his education, whether by books or the arts.

"Look at the guy who's talking to Taylor and Georgina," Sarah said, straightening her sunglasses so she could see better. "Have you ever seen anyone so gorgeous in your life?"

"Not bad," Aurora said, "excuse the cliché, but you'd have to like tall, dark, and handsome." He looked vaguely familiar, but since she'd been back in town, everyone looked vaguely familiar.

"Uh, ye—ah," Sarah said, "and I do." She wanted to hurry over and assist him in whatever he was searching for, but she held back. She'd observe him for a few minutes, enjoy the view, and when he grew closer, look for a wedding ring. "My heart's racing," she whispered.

"My grandmother would have called you 'hot-to-trot.'"

"Hey, I'm thirty-four. My biological clock is like a ticking time-bomb," Sarah said, her eyes riveted on the man.

The man nodded in response to something one of the other women said and strode toward Aurora and Sarah. He was dressed in steel-toe boots, creased jeans, and a crisp, button-down sports shirt. He had a square jaw and Roman nose. When he drew close, he pushed his sunglasses onto the top of a head full of wavy black hair and said, "Which one of you is the owner?"

"Me," Aurora said, raising a hand.

"I'm her BFF." Sarah's endorphins spiked. The man's silver-gray eyes were the color of the bayou when the overhead sun reflected off the water. "Something we can help you with?" She took a minuscule step toward him.

He held out his hand to Aurora. "I'm Ian. I just moved here and bought a house I'm renovating."

"I'm Aurora. Looks like you and a lot of other people in town have the same idea, as do we." Aurora shook his hand, getting a whiff of spicy aftershave. His callused hand dwarfed her tiny one. "I'm not complaining. My husband and I are hoping to clear out our uh—barn—that's what we call the structure behind me—and make a little cash. What are you looking for?"

He glanced at the doors, then the windows positioned under the tree. "Probably a lot of the things you're selling. Where'd all this come from?"

"My grandfather, in his dotage, had a business cleaning up job sites and house demolitions around here and sometimes after move-outs."

Sarah said, "He also liked roaming around town on the weekends when people had estate sales. I'm Sarah." She shook his warm hand before he could put it away. Even as tall as she was, his size overwhelmed her. At his glance, she said, "I'm an old friend of the family. Long story."

"Anyway," Ian said, "I'll go ahead and take a look at what you have. Okay if I let my dog out of my truck and bring him on the property? He's trained."

"What kind of dog?" Sarah asked. "Aurora's a big fan of animals."

"German Shepherd. His name is Gerhard."

"I'll walk with you to your truck," Aurora said. "I want to see him before I agree. A lot of people are scared of big dogs."

"I could go," Sarah said. "You need to stay here to answer your customers' questions."

"Yeah, okay. You'll let me know if you have any concerns." She waved them away.

As soon as Sarah and Ian left, the grouchy man who'd wanted to come in early approached Aurora. His stooped back attested to his advanced age. He clutched a Mason jar of screws in his right hand and one of nails in his left.

Aurora crossed her arms and faked a smile. "May I help you with something?"

"You don't remember me, do you, Ms. Ivy?" The bill of his gimme cap cast shadows over his eyes.

Aurora squinted at him. "No, and it's Morris now. Ivy was my maiden name."

"I was a friend of your grandfather's. I'd shake your hand but mine are full. Name's Hartley. Clint Hartley."

"You do look vaguely familiar, and your name rings a bell. Sorry, it's been a long time."

"I used to go on the hunt for stuff on the weekends with Amos." He held up the containers. "I don't need these screws and nails but want them to remind me of him. Not that I really need reminding. How much?"

Aurora quoted him a few dollars and wracked her brain to remember him. He set down the jars and dug into his pockets for some wrinkled dollar bills. Since she'd moved back to town, almost everywhere she went, people spoke to her, introducing themselves. "I'm happy you remember my grandpa."

"I'll never forget him. Glad you came back to town. Welcome. Are you going to fix up the house or what?"

"Yes, sir. Renovate it. Modernize it, but we want the house to look as much like a farmhouse as possible."

"You and your brother, Harry? Is he moving back here as well?"

"No. My husband and I bought Harold out. He's a city boy now. He'll only be back to visit." She wasn't going to tell him how much Harry hated small-town life, small-town atmosphere.

"That's too bad. I always liked him. What's he doing now?"

"Married with a couple of kids."

"You got any children?"

Aurora weighed how much more of her life she wanted to share with the old man. "Maybe in a few years."

His eyes ran up and down her body. "You're what we used to call getting-kinda-long-in-the-tooth. I thought you girls wanted to have kids before your mid-thirties."

Now he was getting too personal. "Women are having kids later now. So anyway ..."

He chuckled. "None of my business. So, what about the rest of the stuff back there in the—"

"Barn? We'll keep having sales until it's empty, or no one comes back to buy anything. Then we'll probably tear the old building down." She glanced toward the barn.

"Wouldn't hurt anyone's feelings if you did. Well, guess I'll be seeing you around town. Nice talking to you."

"Yes, sir. Thanks for speaking with me." This time, her smile wasn't fake. He seemed like a nice old man, even if he was nosy. She was about to head inside to see if she could be of any help to anyone and make sure they hadn't taken down her tape barrier when Sarah and Ian came walking back. Ian led a huge, black-and-tan German shepherd on a leash.

"Ian has a truck just like Jeff's," Sarah said. "Exactly like Jeff's."

"What a coincidence," Aurora said, knowing there existed thousands of white trucks in the area. "This is Gerhard? He's ginormous. How old is he?"

"Three. I've had him since he was a puppy. Would you like to meet him?" Ian squatted down next to Gerhard and crooked his finger at Aurora, who crouched down, careful not to get too near or hover over the dog.

Gerhard sniffed Aurora from a distance and took a couple of steps closer, sniffing some more, his cold nose grazing her arm.

Aurora smiled at Gerhard and held out her hand. Gerhard licked her hand and looked at her.

Ian said, "Gerhard, shake hands."

The dog sat back and lifted his right paw, pointing in Aurora's direction.

"Look at him. I think he likes me. He's grinning." Aurora shook Gerhard's paw. "I guess it's okay for me to pet him now?"

Ian stood. "Sure."

Aurora scratched under Gerhard's chin for a few moments and slowly moved to stroke his head. His fur was warm and soft. He put a paw on her shoulder.

"Amazing," Sarah said. "Aurora's always had a way with animals."

"I had a German Shepherd when I was a tiny girl. Her name was Heidi."

"Good morning," a voice behind them said.

Jeff walked toward them, a steaming coffee mug in his right fist. He wore a plain white T-shirt, revealing his bulging biceps, and tight faded jeans. Wraparound sunglasses covered his eyes. His undercut dishwater blond hair was shorter than Ian's on top but in need of a trim along the sides. "Hi honey," he said, his bright smile not quite reaching his eyes.

Aurora, feeling ire on her tongue, did the obligatory kiss thing on Jeff's cheek only because he'd notice, otherwise. "Hey, sleepyhead, we can use your help." She didn't meet his eyes, not wanting him to be able to read anything in hers.

Jeff's eyes cut from her to Sarah and landed on Ian. "I'm Jeff Morris." He switched his mug to his left hand and held out his right.

"Ian Rawlings." He shook Jeff's hand. "This is Gerhard. Sit, Gerhard."

"Ian's renovating a house, too," Aurora said. "He's probably going to use a lot of Grandpa's stuff."

Jeff slung his arm around Aurora's shoulders. "Oh yeah? Where's your house located?"

"Two blocks off Main." Ian pointed over his shoulder. "A couple of miles from here."

"Everything's a couple of miles from here." Jeff grinned. "Farm-house or what?"

"Two-story Victorian. Needs a lot of work. Somebody got to it a while back and just about ruined it, putting in builder-grade windows and doors—you probably know what I'm talking about. It'll take some time to put it to rights."

"Depending on how you look at it, we got lucky. Aurora's grand-parents never updated this place much, though they added a small room years ago. That's going to need fixing. What do you do for a living, Ian?"

Gerhard stirred. "I'm going to have to put Gerhard back in the truck. Too many people here now."

Aurora said, "I don't want him to scare people, either. He's awfully big even if he is sweet. I can take him if you tell me where you're parked. He and I can get better acquainted." She looked at the dog. "Can't we, Gerhard? Or," she said to Ian, "since your truck is like Jeff's, I can probably find it."

Sarah said, "Funny, right Jeff? But I guess there are a lot of white pickups in Texas."

"Millions," Jeff said.

"You sure you want to take him?" Ian asked Aurora, holding out the leash. "It's not locked, and the window's down enough for him to stick his head out."

"I'm sure. We can get some exercise, huh, Gerhard?" Aurora took the leash and shrugged out of Jeff's arm, tapping his middle as she crossed in front of him, restraining herself from punching his stomach. "Back in a minute." She led Gerhard in a jog toward the street.

Jeff's eyes followed Aurora before turning back to Ian. "So, what do you do?"

Sarah glanced over at Taylor, standing near the entrance to the barn and beckoning to her.

"I renovate houses," Ian said. "I guess you could call it flipping them, but really, I love working with my hands. I buy older homes, historical ones if I can find them, and live in them while I'm fixing them up. You might think it's weird, but as an army brat, I got used to moving a lot. When I sell the renovated house, I move to another place."

"So, you're new in our little town?" Sarah asked. "I don't believe I've ever run into you before today." She would have remembered for sure.

Jeff raised an eyebrow. "You scout houses while you're fixing one, sell it, and then move on to another town? You must spend some time on the road."

"Occasionally, it takes me a while to find a house I want, so yeah. Once I've got the current one in progress, maybe half through, I begin my physical search. Of course, these days, I can do preliminary searches online." Ian shrugged. "Maybe someday I'll settle down. Not any time soon, though."

Sarah said, "You must get lonely, sometimes, don't you? How many houses do you renovate in a town before you move on?"

Ian's eyes rested on Sarah's face for a moment, as if he had just seen her. "One. I can take up to six months, or more, depending on the house. I usually find a way to entertain myself even in the smallest of towns."

"Seems like an unusual way to make a living," Sarah said. Over his shoulder, she spotted Taylor still beckoning to her.

Jeff cocked his head. "It sure does."

"Where do you work?" Ian asked, hooking a thumb in his belt loop. His stance became more rigid.

"Medical sales." Jeff stood taller and sipped from his coffee cup. After a moment, he said, "Worked my way up to manager, but I still have a territory. I like the work and the travel. Aurora's not always happy with my schedule, or lack of one sometimes, but I like the variety."

Aurora jogged back toward them. "He's just the sweetest dog. I bet he's good company."

"He is." Ian side-stepped toward the barn. "I'd better look at your materials before it's all spoken for."

Sarah said, "Aurora, Ian moves around a lot. He renovates a house and then moves to another town and does another one."

Aurora said, "Yes, your point is?"

"You know how there was another woman's body discovered this morning?" Sarah threw a faux grin at Jeff. "You haven't been out here long enough to hear the news, Jeff." Sarah turned her eyes on Ian. "There have been several women killed in this neck of the woods. I was just thinking. Aurora writes mysteries, Ian."

"What's that got to do with anything?" Aurora asked.

"How Ian makes a living would be great cover for a serial killer."

"Sarah!" Aurora whacked her friend on the arm.

Jeff's face blanched. "Damn, Sarah."

Ian's eyes flared. He gritted his teeth.

20

Aurora said, "That's not even funny. What would make you say a thing like that?"

"I was just kidding. I was thinking in your next book you could have a serial killer, and men with jobs like Ian's or like truck drivers, could be suspects because of how they work."

"My mystery is a who-dun-it, Sarah. I don't think serial killers are in who-dun-its."

"What a strange thing to say." Ian's jaw flexed. He gave Sarah the side eye and shook his head. "I'm definitely going to look around now." He strode in the direction of the windows under the tree. Glancing at the threesome behind him, a frown on his face and an eyebrow arched, he shook his head again.

Sarah called after him, "Nice meeting you, Ian." She shrugged at Aurora and Jeff. "I'm sorry. I thought y'all would laugh. I've got to get to work, too." She hurried across the yard toward Taylor.

"I need your help," Taylor said, her eyes darting to where Aurora and Jeff still stood. "What was going on over there between Jeff and the other big guy?"

"From the looks of it, Jeff and Ian were sizing each other up. You should have seen them giving each other the once-over."

"His name's Ian? He's got a lot going for him."

"Yeah, he does. I'd like to get to know him better, but I think I blew it."

"What'd you do?"

"Oh, I made an offhand remark about how he could be a serial killer."

Taylor rolled her eyes. "What? You're going to have to explain that to me, but before you do, can you stand here and make sure no one digs through the stuff on the other side of the crime scene tape while I run inside to use the bathroom?"

"Sure." Sarah stood at the entrance to the barn like a security guard watching suspicious characters, feet spread, hands on hips. Ian walked inside but kept his distance from her. Across the yard, Aurora shook her head and frowned. Jeff's shoulders were up around his ears as he spoke to Aurora, a sure sign he was tense. Wouldn't be the first time Sarah had been on the wrong side of Jeff. She didn't want Aurora to be angry, though. They'd just grown close again since the couple had moved back to town. She'd try to talk to Aurora later. Their "girls' afternoon" on Monday would be a good time, after they'd all had a glass of wine or two.

CHAPTER

THREE

Monday was another windy, but bright, fall morning with few clouds overhead. If the weather held, the temperature might remain in the high 80s. Starting at six-thirty, Aurora glued herself to her desk chair in the cramped third bedroom of the farmhouse. Her grandparents had hastily added the room when Aurora and Harry moved in with them. Once she and Jeff took possession of the house, they'd agreed the little room would be her office. As usual, she wore an old pair of jeans, a stained T-shirt, and thin sandals. The cooling in the back of the house left a lot to be desired as would the heating once the temperature dropped.

She worked on her book in progress or, as Aurora and many writers called it, her WIP. Work in Progress. Her goal was to maintain a schedule of writing for a minimum of two hours every weekday morning before she took on any other tasks. She'd made a schedule and pinned it on a cork bulletin board on the wall next to her desk

Weekends were reserved for time with Jeff and projects other than her writing. If nothing else was on her weekday schedule, Aurora might even work until her rear end became numb. After her divorce, she had spent most of her weekends writing, since she didn't have much of a life outside of the classroom. Once her relationship with Jeff began, Aurora had to change some activities. Hard to write and court, one of her old instructors had told her. Two hours a day, though, enabled her to get a lot done. She was content with her routine and hoped to finish her first book soon.

Her project was a who-dun-it mystery. She'd done a stream of consciousness synopsis and, later, an outline. She had been afraid of making up the story as she went—which she had learned was called a pantser—worrying she'd never come out with an organized story. Now, she was revising the outline and had just begun the narrative after writing summaries for each chapter, subject to change, of course. Euphoria filled her every time she sat down in front of her computer.

Aurora volunteered at the animal shelter most Mondays. Today, when she pulled her Prius into the parking lot, Taylor stood at the glass door entrance. Aurora had been a volunteer long enough to know Taylor shadowing the doorway meant something was amiss. Her somber face didn't disabuse Aurora of that notion.

The County Animal Shelter had begun as a temporary solution to a major problem many years earlier. Packs of dogs had roamed the neighborhoods, especially in the most rural areas where people kept farm animals like rabbits, or chickens, or turkeys, and even goats. In the middle of the night, dogs would kill whatever animal they could find. Rabbits, especially, had been their favorites, the dogs mystifyingly getting ahold of them and pulling them through the holes in the cages. The invasions into the henhouses were not as violent and bloody, but still too regular and costly. People told of hearing squawks and cries. Animals screamed and howled. Back then, if residents saw any dogs out and about without an owner, they'd put them down. Thinking about it, could she have heard an animal crying out a few nights earlier when she'd been awakened?

Over the years, attitudes had become more compassionate. Some folks moved into town and began campaigning against cruelty to animals. Eventually, the shelter had been established, a twenty-by-thirty metal building, which had expanded over the years and had sections for cats, sections for dogs, a small section for the other animals, offices, and even a little kitchen.

Now, Taylor held the front door open, pungent animal odors wafting past her. She wore black jeans, a pullover cotton sweater, and tan Crocs over animal-print socks. She pounced as soon as Aurora cleared the entrance. "Come into the back, the vet's work area." Taylor, who started out as a volunteer while in high school and college, had been appointed executive director almost as soon as she graduated, when the volunteer director saw an opportunity to beg off. Taylor's life's work was caring for unfortunate animals.

"Let me at least put my purse down," Aurora said, resisting Taylor's tug on her arm. Aurora staffed the front desk part of the time, the remainder she spent helping take care of the animals. "Hey, Sissy," she said to the young woman on the phone at the front desk. After popping her purse into the back of a file cabinet behind one of the front desks, Aurora followed Taylor into the dog section. The dogs' barking became more insistent as soon as the women approached.

Aurora's heart turned inside out whenever she witnessed the large number of animals waiting to be adopted. Each time she volunteered, she hoped to see a decrease in the population. She had to resist the urge to take the animals home. Jeff didn't want a dog. A cat either. Or even a bird or a gerbil. He'd said he didn't have time for a pet and didn't want to take care of one. What he really wanted was for Aurora to get pregnant, but so far she'd been able to put him off.

Taylor led Aurora to a small office where normally the vet functioned, though the vet wasn't present. They stopped at the counter centered in the room, a small box sitting on top, a tiny black and white furball curled up inside.

"Awwww," Aurora said. "What a sweet little pup."

"The sheriff's office raided a house over the weekend and found starving horses out back, dogs in filthy pens, and too many cats to count both inside the house and roaming the back acres. This little baby was in a pen with its dead mother, who was just as skinny, and two other puppies who were also dead. Looked like they starved to death."

Aurora's eyes welled up. "I can't stand when people do that." She looked at the little mutt who was sleeping, its tummy faintly rising and falling as it breathed. "Male or female?"

"Female. Doesn't she just break your heart?"

"You know it does. What do you think she is? Looks like part poodle."

"Couldn't be standard poodle and not even a miniature, I don't think. Not big enough. Doctor Al thinks she's probably a doxiepoo, or another small mix, though it's hard to tell when she's in such a poor condition. He thinks the pup is probably three months old but hasn't grown properly because of neglect."

"She's so little. She could be a teacup." Aurora stroked the puppy's back.

"The doc thinks she'll grow somewhat larger once she's properly fed and taken care of. Right now, she needs constant attention and small bits of food, until she can tolerate regular puppy size servings, and a lot of love."

The puppy squeaked and sighed. Aurora's heart wrenched. "Awww, listen to her. She's probably dreaming."

"Probably having a nightmare," Taylor said through clenched teeth. "I hope they keep that woman in jail."

"The one who had all the animals?"

"She's charged with animal cruelty. I hope they throw the book at her."

"Yeah, me too. I don't understand why people do this when they can surrender them so easily." She sighed herself.

"So, anyway, Aurora, among other things, the reason I wanted you to see this puppy is Ronnie is on vacation, which has left us short... I don't have enough people to give this baby the kind of care she needs."

Aurora took a step back, glancing from Taylor to the puppy.

"I need someone to foster her. Someone who could watch over her constantly, feed her special food at least five times a day until she's up to eating regular food, and someone who would love her and pet her and take good care of her until she's well enough to be adopted. In sum, I need you."

Aurora rocked on her heels. "I—uh—"

"We would provide the special food, of course."

Aurora rubbed her lips together and started to respond. "I—"

"Look, I know Jeff doesn't like animals." Taylor had put on her best pleading expression—wrinkled brow, pleading eyes.

"It isn't that he doesn't like animals—"

Taylor cocked her head. "That's not what you said before."

"I said when I told him I wanted a dog, he said he'd rather try again for a baby. I never said he didn't like animals. We talked about getting a dog or cat once we were really settled."

"I don't want to argue with you. I just thought since he's gone so often, and since you work from home, you'd be the ideal person to foster this furbaby for a little while. At least until I can find someone else. He wouldn't object if it was just temporary, would he?"

Aurora wasn't sure she wanted to get into a discussion with Jeff over a sick puppy. He might argue if she could care for a puppy, she could care for a baby. She looked at the puppy again. "How long are you thinking it'll be until she's adoptable?"

Taylor stroked her chin, her eyes squinting. "A month? Two months? Maybe less if I find someone else to foster her."

Or more, Aurora thought, her stomach quivering. "Can I have this afternoon to think it over? I'm not promising. I just want to think about it."

"Sure. In the meantime," Taylor scooped up the puppy, "would you feed her now? I know she's sleeping, but the doc gave me a schedule. It's time for her to eat." She settled the puppy in Aurora's hands.

"I know what you're doing," Aurora said, taking the puppy and running her fingers over its soft little head. "I'll feed her and take care of her today, but I'm still going to think it over." Jeff's schedule required him to be out of town until Friday. She could, at least, tend to the puppy until then. "She's so sweet. She's not rooting around like a newborn, but you can tell from her body language she's looking for something."

"I set up a little station for you over here." Taylor pointed to a corner where a wooden rocking chair with a flowered cushion and a small table laden with a bag of prescription puppy food were positioned. An eye dropper, a little water dish filled with water, some newspaper to catch the pup's waste, and a baby blanket were all ready for someone to sit there with the pup. A small glass of lemonade waited for Aurora.

"I won't be suckered in. I'll take care of the puppy this afternoon and mull it over. Don't think you've convinced me."

"Thank you for being such a good friend and such a good volunteer."

"Get out of here before I change my mind." Shaking her head, Aurora turned her attention to the black and white creature cupped in her hands. Swallowing some tart lemonade, she made herself comfortable with the lump of a pup. She'd worry about any consequences later.

CHAPTER
FOUR

Aurora's wooden porch had a deep overhang and a rail running down the side of the farmhouse. In warm weather, she liked to sit outside and contemplate the world. The threat of rain had cleared off, unfortunately, since there had been a long dry spell, but the clouds had caused the temperature to drop enough to almost feel comfortable and a slight breeze to blow. Aside from the dust the wind had whipped up, resulting in that gritty taste if one breathed too deeply, sitting on the porch was enjoyable. She could only hope that soon rain would bring freshness to the yard, afterward the tree leaves glistening in the sun.

Once Aurora and Jeff had moved back to town, and Jeff's job took him away, Aurora and her friends started a routine of meeting on Monday evenings on her porch. Now, the puppy and a baby blanket lay in a box next to her chair. In quick succession, the other women began to arrive.

Taylor came with another woman in tow. "Aurora, do you remember Monica? I brought her again."

"Come on in, Monica. I thought we'd made you welcome last

Monday, but if not, welcome. You can come anytime. You don't need Taylor to bring you."

"All right now," Taylor said, her eyes flashing with humor. "I'm going into the kitchen to open my wine and get some glasses."

"Sit down here next to me, Monica, and let's get better acquainted."

"Thank you," Monica said. "This is great for porch sitting." Monica had naturally curly blonde hair that had not grown darker as she'd grown older, pale green eyes, and a rosebud mouth. She was almost six feet tall and paper thin. She wore pink scrubs.

"Yep, and you don't have to be formal. If I remember correctly, you work at the hospital?"

"Respiratory therapist."

"Then you probably know my husband, Jeff. "

"I've seen him around, but I don't know him. Medical sales, right?"

"Yes. Are you married? I'm just wondering. Don't want to make this sound like the third degree."

Monica pulled her phone from her pocket and scrolled for a few moments. "This is a picture of my husband and daughter."

Aurora took the phone. "What a nice looking man. And your daughter is beautiful. What is she, about eight?"

"Third grade. And Tommy's a firefighter."

Aurora handed the phone back. "What a body. He looks like he could be on the shelter's firefighter calendar."

"You ought to see him with no clothes on." Monica slapped her own cheek. "Can't believe I said that."

Aurora said, "Hey, maybe next year he can be on the calendar where we can all enjoy looking at him. They put it out for the benefit of the Humane Society."

"I know. Taylor told me. I'm definitely going to ask him. I don't mind sharing as long as women look and don't touch." She put her phone away. "How long have y'all been married?"

"Not long. A few months."

Monica's eyes flickered to the lump in the box next to Aurora's chair. "Is that the puppy I heard about?"

"Yes. Want to see her?" Aurora lifted the blanket. "You can stroke her head, but please don't pick her up. I don't think it's good for her to be handled by a lot of different people when she's this young and in bad shape."

Monica kneeled and brushed her forefinger over the puppy's head. "She's so tiny and soft."

"She could be the runt of the litter, or just little because she almost starved to death. I'm surprised she didn't die like the rest of them and their mother. Taylor probably told you about that."

"So sad. I don't know why people do stuff like that. If you can't take care of an animal, find someone who can." The puppy squirmed and let out a mini-sigh. Monica sat back down. "I've been volunteering at the shelter, too. I take Ava sometimes. She likes to hold the kittens and helps clean the cages."

"Ava, that's your daughter?"

"She thinks she wants to be a vet when she grows up."

Taylor pushed the door open with her foot. "Wine for all of us." She held three glasses of white wine, offering one to each of them. The screen door banged behind her.

"Hey, thanks," Aurora said. "Monica and I are getting better acquainted. We'll probably see each other at the shelter." She sniffed the wine and took a sip. "Not too sweet but so good."

Taylor took the chair on the other side of Aurora. "I'm trying to talk Monica into fostering, too. Right, Monica?"

Monica said, "Yeah. I'm thinking about it. Don't pressure me."

"I know how she does that." Aurora's eyes shifted to Taylor.

Sarah arrived and hurried into the kitchen without even a greeting. Aurora had wanted to talk to Sarah alone, but it didn't look like that was going to happen today.

Georgina arrived last, breathless like she'd run from the police station. She still wore her police uniform, but the shirt hung out over the waist band. "Wait 'til I tell you the news." She held up a finger.

"Let me get a glass first and make a pit stop." She set a plate of vegetables and dip on the table and hurried inside.

"Wonder what that was about," Monica said from the porch railing where she now perched.

The others shrugged.

"Before Georgina gets back, I want to hear about your sale last weekend," Monica said. She shrugged out of a lightweight blue sweater and hung it next to her. "Sorry I couldn't make it. I'm hoping the next time you have a sale, I won't have anything else planned. Did y'all make a lot of money?"

"Money wasn't our main goal, though we did okay," Aurora said. "We got rid of a lot of the reusable material we didn't want and met some new people." She glanced at the door where Sarah had gone and cringed inside as she remembered what Jeff had said after Sarah had put her foot in her mouth.

"What was that about?" he'd asked, his eyes following Sarah when she'd left to see what Taylor wanted.

"I can't always explain Sarah's behavior even if she's been a lifelong friend."

"You'd better talk to her, Aurora. Shooting her mouth off like that is not exactly how to keep friends. I hope no one, including that guy, Ian, thinks talking like that is okay."

"She was trying to be funny, I think maybe she was trying to come up with conversation to engage that guy, Ian."

"I saw how she looked at him, but that's not exactly how to get the right kind of attention."

"I feel sorry for her." Aurora had taken Jeff's arm and squeezed it. "I was lucky enough to find you. Second time's the charm."

Jeff's shoulders loosened as he relaxed his stiff pose. "I'm going to move some more things out of the barn." He handed his coffee mug to her and kissed her on the cheek. "Put this on the porch for me."

Aurora crab-walked the mug to the porch, watching as Jeff passed by Sarah, who appeared not to see him.

Now, Aurora felt grateful they'd been so busy over the weekend that Jeff had apparently forgotten the incident with Sarah. He hadn't mentioned it again before he'd left to go back to work. She so wanted them to be friends, to at least try to like each other.

When Sarah returned, wineglass filled with red, she said, "Monica, I'm glad you're married so you won't give me any competition. There was this really cute—no, handsome—man who henceforth I shall refer to as HM—who came here Saturday. He's not from here." She took the chair Monica had abandoned.

"He renovates houses," Taylor said, shifting in her chair so she could see their faces. "Moves around from town-to-town, fixes up a house, sells it, and moves on."

"I'm telling it, Taylor," Sarah said and let out something akin to a giggle. "Wait until you see him, Monica. He's wet-your-pants-good-looking."

"He's probably gay," Monica said.

"I don't think so," Sarah said. "I caught him giving me the once-over."

"That was after you made that rude comment," Aurora said.

Sarah ignored her. "Anyway, I'm going to be on the look-out for him. I might even drive around town and try to find the house he's working on."

"What comment?" Monica asked but received no reply.

"You can't be that desperate," Aurora said, stroking the top of the pup's head in response to a tiny sigh.

"Yes, I can," Sarah said. "These days if you don't assert yourself, you lose out. The men expect you to call them. They don't always want to be the one to reach out first."

"Where'd you hear that?" Monica asked.

"I read it on the Internet. There's a lot of stuff online about dating. You wouldn't believe it."

"I'd believe it," Taylor said. "There are probably YouTube videos about it, too."

Sarah slapped the table, causing the wine to ripple in the glasses perched on it. "There're millions of them. Did you know there are dating coaches? But they're expensive."

"You checked one out?" Aurora asked.

Sarah ducked her head. "Well, yeah, I've been thinking about signing up with one."

"So, you are that desperate," Monica said. She gave Sarah a faux frown.

Sarah gulped some red wine. "Easy to joke about it, but especially in small towns like this one, men—good men—are scarce."

"What?" Georgina said from the doorway, drying her hands on a paper towel. "What are y'all talking about? Men again?"

"Well, Sarah is, anyway," Aurora said.

"There's not a shortage, if you know where to find them," Georgina said, shaking her head. She peeled back the plastic wrap covering the tray she'd brought, and the aroma of garlic filled the air. "Try these olives I found." She popped one into her mouth and chased it with a swallow of white wine.

"Not for you," Sarah said. "You work at the P.D. There're all kinds of men there, and in the S.O., the sheriff's office, coming in and out all day long."

Georgina shrugged. "Seems like lately most of them are married or getting a divorce. I wouldn't want to be anyone's rebound person." She glanced Aurora's way.

"You talking about me?" Aurora asked. "I don't consider Jeff to be my rebound person."

"You did get married fast," Sarah said. "Anyway, Georgina, you couldn't have a better job to meet men than as a police officer."

"Well, probably there are better jobs, but I can't think of any at the moment. When I do, I'll let you know." Georgina dragged up a vacant chair from further down the porch. She unbuttoned the top two buttons on her shirt and ran her fingers through her hair. "Whew. Long day."

"What were you going to tell us when you arrived?" Aurora asked. "You said you had some news."

"Oh, yeah, news about the body of that woman they found last Friday."

"Gruesome," Sarah said. "Not sure I want to hear the sordid details."

Georgina ignored Sarah. "We all need to know what's going on if we're to protect ourselves."

"Don't listen to Sarah," Monica said. "I, at least, want to know. My husband heard something and was asking me if I'd heard about it."

"Well," Georgina said, her eyes sweeping around the circle of women as if she were trying to create suspense, "I told some of you about it on Saturday. But she was found on the side of the road near here. They think she might be another victim of that serial killer."

"Give us the deets," Taylor said.

"Looks like she was hit by a car or a truck."

"Then it can't be a serial killer," Aurora said. "Why would they think she was killed by a serial killer?"

The women all leaned toward Georgina, like kids listening to ghost stories around a campfire.

"First, from what I've heard so far, there was no reason for her to be out on that road. She didn't live near us. So why was she out there?"

"Where was her car?" Sarah asked.

"Her SUV. At a mall. They found it this morning. Her purse was sitting on the front seat."

"They think somebody snatched her while she was getting into her car?" Taylor asked.

Georgina nodded. "They think she was taken in the middle of the afternoon and assaulted all night and thrown out on the road early in the morning."

The women began speaking at once.

"And then run over?"

"Did anyone see a white panel truck or van? You always hear

about the bad guys having trucks or vans that don't have any windows on the sides," Sarah said.

"So, he would have, what, knocked her out and then run over her?"

Georgina said, "They're doing an autopsy and will look for any other signs of how she might have died."

"He could have thrown her out in the road in the dark and another vehicle hit her and ran over her."

"Who was it? Have they identified her yet?"

"I hope we didn't know her."

"I don't know why we would. They know her ID, but I couldn't find out yet." Georgina took a sip of her wine. "As soon as I hear, y'all will be the first to know."

"Makes me afraid to go shopping," Taylor said.

"We don't know that she was from anywhere around here, though. She could have been a tourist. She could have been stalked at the mall and grabbed when she came out. She could have been thrown out here by the person—like he was passing through and threw out a litter of kittens," Sarah said.

Aurora's eyes were fixed on Sarah, but she didn't comment.

Taylor grimaced. "I hate it when people throw out kittens and puppies like they're so much trash."

Again, several of them chimed in.

"Gruesome."

"Poor lady."

"I vote we shop together for a while, like Girl Scouts always going with a buddy," Aurora said. "Maybe not Taylor because she works out and could probably handle herself but most of the rest of us—"

"Thanks a lot," Taylor said.

"I'm packing," Monica said. "I keep my gun in my purse except when I'm in places like a parking lot by myself."

"Like you'd be able to get it out in time if some big old guy grabbed you," Georgina said.

"I take it out of my purse before I leave the store," Monica said, checking the other women's faces to see if anyone agreed with her.

"I already carry a gun," Taylor said.

They all turned to her. She shrugged.

Aurora said, "So y'all have guns in your purses right now?" She glanced at each of their faces.

"Of course. I have an idea," said Georgina. "Let's all put tracker apps on our phones, so we can keep tabs on each other. That way, at least, if one of us gets snatched, we can track her phone."

Taylor pulled her phone from her shoulder bag and tapped on the screen.

"That's a little extreme, don't you think?" Sarah asked.

"No." Georgina was the only one of them who worked around the criminal justice system. She was a party to conversations between other police officers as they came and went, in addition to the cases of her own she fielded every day. She stared down Sarah and the others. "Don't forget this victim is only one of several over the last year or so."

"Not just in our county," Monica said.

"No, in the Gulf Coast area and surrounding counties, plus Montgomery County, which isn't even on the coast. Victims have been missing or killed all over." Georgina's face had grown red. "And some of the other victims were also found on a roadside or nearby."

"Those are the counties most of us travel around in when we're shopping or whatever," Taylor said.

Their tone had grown somber and quiet. A bird twittered down by the bayou. A gentle breeze blew the women's hair across their faces. A faint squeal came from down by Aurora's feet, followed by a puppy sigh. She said, "When I look at helpless animals—or children —or even old people, I want to do something to make the world safer."

"You can add women to that list," Taylor said.

"You can add people in general to that list," Georgina said.

"That's the reason I wanted to be a cop. Seems like there's violence everywhere, all the shootings, like a worldwide war zone."

"Um-hum," several of the women uttered at the same time, nodding.

"Let's change the subject to something more cheerful," Monica said. She poured herself another glass of wine. "When are y'all going to be ready to have another sale, Aurora? And what can we do to help?"

Two hours later when all the women except Sarah had departed, she and Aurora straightened up the porch before taking the puppy inside. They dumped the leftovers and settled down at the kitchen table. Aurora held the puppy in her lap and stroked its little head. "Thanks for staying a few minutes longer."

Sarah said, "I could tell all evening something is wrong. You want to just come out and tell me or beat around the bush for a few minutes?"

"I think Jeff is having an affair."

Sarah straightened her spine. She closed one eye and looked sideways at Aurora. "No way. Y'all haven't even been married, what, three months? The honeymoon can't be over yet."

Aurora expelled a gust of air and nodded. "I think it's true."

"What makes you think so?"

"When we were dating, he would have some late nights on the road, so I knew what his schedule would be like if we married."

"And he still has late nights on the road, right?"

"But more and more, it seems. Sometimes really late. Like last Friday, he didn't get home until after two a.m."

"Well, couldn't he have been coming home from really far away?"

"That's what he says every time. But I'm sure I smelled a woman's perfume on his clothes."

"Maybe whoever he called on was over-perfumed," Sarah said, her face drawn up in skepticism.

"See, even you don't believe that. He'd have to get really close to someone for his clothes to smell like them."

"And you recognize that because of—"

"Having experienced this with my ex and my ex-best friend." Aurora squeezed her eyes shut and shook her head. "I can't go through that again. I *won't*."

Sarah crossed her arms and sat back. "What are you going to do?"

"I'm not going to make an appointment with a lawyer like he's asked me to do." Aurora rose and began pacing, the puppy ensconced under one arm.

"To put the house in both names, you mean?"

"He's been pressing me to do that and to make wills leaving everything to each other." She huffed. "And to see an insurance agent about life insurance for me. He has some with his company."

Sarah cocked her head in a wary look. "I wouldn't either. That bothers me that he wants you to do all that already when you've only been married for a short time."

Aurora stopped and fixed her eyes on Sarah. "That just gave me goosebumps." She rubbed her arms.

Sarah's eyes flared. "Are you going to try to find out what he's up to?"

"You have any suggestions?"

"You can't follow him all over God's creation, that's for sure. You could search his truck when he's sleeping, or if he takes y'all's junker truck to the dump."

Aurora's eyes welled up with tears. "I can't believe I'm finding myself in this situation again. He was so sweet to me and understanding of my situation. I thought this would be different." She pulled a paper towel from the roll and rubbed her eyes with it.

Sarah put an arm around her friend. "I know, honey. But be patient. Maybe there's a reasonable explanation. All you have right now is a smell."

Nodding, Aurora said, "I've been trying to think back to when we were dating and whether I noticed any scent on his clothes then. I don't remember, which may not mean anything. I was so pleased to have such a good-looking man pay attention to me."

"Awwww..." Sarah squeezed Aurora's shoulders.

"I've been writing in my journal about his schedule and all. Maybe I'll figure out a way to, heck, figure out what he's doing and with whom."

"You will. In the meantime, I wanted to tell you *I have* figured out where HM lives."

"HM? Oh, Handsome Man. Ian. I can't believe you." A small smile broke out on her lips.

"I thought about it, and we don't know anything about him. I was joking the other day, but what if he is the killer?"

Aurora laughed. "I guess that'll give you something exciting in your life other than grading papers. So, you check him out, and I'll try to keep tabs on my husband, and we can compare notes."

"It's a deal." Sarah held up her palm to they could slap hands, which they did. Both shrugged and laughed, and Sarah left.

Aurora, on the other hand, sat staring into space, intent on coming up with a plan. No way was she going to go through the same experience with Jeff that she did with the first husband.

CHAPTER
FIVE

O n Tuesday, Aurora spent the morning working on her novel. Though her original plan had been to make it a who-dun-it mystery, she kind of liked what Sarah had said, maybe a who-dun-it mystery with an off-stage serial killer, but the serial killer is someone the main character knows? After lunch, she put the pup in a basket to take out to the barn, so she wouldn't have to worry while she was sorting things for the next sale.

Standing in the entrance, Aurora visually divided the barn's contents into thirds. She'd attack the left side, leaving the right with its barrier formed by tall two-by-fours and one-by-tens for Jeff. They could work their way to the center.

After pushing the wheelbarrow inside, Aurora pulled down the yellow crime scene tape left from Saturday. She began throwing in useless pieces of wood and unidentifiable, at least to her, pieces of metal until the wheelbarrow was as full as she thought she could handle. Their old work truck sat in the driveway, so she emptied the wheelbarrow contents into a large cardboard box in the back of the pickup. Jeff had set it up for her to fill and take to the dumpsite.

The work was tedious, but Jeff had asked her to take her best shot, "*If you can spare the time from your book writing and hanging out with your friends.*" He'd smiled and laughed and given her a hug, yet she had detected an undertone. If her complying with his request would make him happy, she'd certainly apply herself.

Digging through a new pile of junk back in the barn, Aurora came across another animal skeleton, one larger than the small rabbit's skull they'd found Saturday morning. Maybe a jackrabbit's. She shrugged and tossed it into the wheelbarrow. A flurry of excitement invaded her chest when she thought of what else she might find amongst Grandfather's treasures.

Once she cleared away boxes stacked one upon another, digging through the sticky spider webs and dusting the dirt off each item she deemed worth keeping, she uncovered some odd pieces of furniture. In the only drawer of a credenza, sans desk, were pens with faded custom logos, pencil stubs, scraps of paper, and even a spiral note-book containing what looked like the beginning of a story. Even with the off-putting smell of dust and decay, Aurora set the items aside for later. A pair of glasses, cheaters she decided after wiping the grit from them and peering through the plastic lenses, lay under the green notebook, along with an outdated cell phone, the glass smashed in the center. The owner of those materials could have been a mystery writer, like her.

Finding an old lamp with its plug intact, Aurora added it to the pile. Later, she'd clean it off and take it inside. If it worked, maybe she could use it somewhere in the house. By mid-afternoon, she hadn't even sorted through a quarter of the left side. If she'd stop examining each piece, she'd make a lot more progress. But could she be expected to just pile old books and magazines in boxes to set out for the sale? No way. There might be something good, some article or story she'd want to read. A desk chair, old but wheels still turning, could be something they'd keep in the future garage once it was built. Assuming there was a future *they*. She intended to work hard to make sure there would be.

"Hey, am I interrupting?" Ian's deep melodic voice resonated throughout the barn, startling Aurora who flinched and shivered before turning toward him. He stood in the entryway.

Laughing, she set a box of hinges aside and stood to face him. "You scared the heck out of me." She didn't really give credence to Sarah's imagination, but his voice did send a shockwave through her.

He wore a wide-eyed expression himself, his eyes riveted on her torso. He was dressed in work boots, tight jeans, a tight, white T-shirt, and a pair of reflecting sunglasses. "Okay if I come in? I mean, is your husband home? If not, do you think he would mind me stopping by to scope out more materials?"

"He's out of town most of this week." Why did she tell him that? Too late, but she felt stupid. "Sure, you can come inside. No problem." The vague impression she knew him from somewhere else still lingered.

He tucked his keys in his pocket. "Where's Jeff off to this week? Will he be gone all week?"

Aurora shrugged. Should she answer his questions? Damn Sarah for making her nervous about the guy. "I don't know where he went this week. I should, but I don't. My bad for not listening—if he even said." She looked down at her old, ripped jeans— ripped further than the original designer intended them to be, higher up, a crew-necked faded cotton T-shirt she'd been given years earlier when she'd participated in a 5K run, and her oldest, worn-out tennis shoes.

"What—What do you have in the basket? You have a baby? No, too small. Something's moving under the blanket. What is it?" He squatted.

She crouched down, too. "A puppy. A tiny rescue Taylor talked me into fostering. You met Taylor last Saturday, I think." Aurora pulled the blanket back.

"I did." He stroked the pup's head.

Could he be a bad guy if he liked puppies? And he had a dog, anyway. A well-trained dog, if she recalled, and she did. "Taylor's the director of the Humane Society. I'm a volunteer. She persuaded me to take care of this baby for a while."

"What a sweetheart. Did your dog object when you brought the puppy home?" He stepped back and looked into Aurora's eyes.

Was he flirting with her? He knew she was married. Or for some reason was he wondering whether she had a dog? "I don't have any pets right now. I'm lobbying my husband for a dog, but I want a fully grown rescue animal." She didn't feel threatened. Ian was just being friendly. But maybe she should be scared. Being home alone would sit easier with her if she had a big dog. She cleared her throat. "Anyhoo—what can I do for you?"

"Oh—um—I've been working on my house. I spotted some wood trim last Saturday when I was here. There's sure to be other things. I hate to buy new stuff if you have some more you want to get rid of." He glanced at her pile of keepers for a moment.

"I haven't made much headway since the sale. I've separated what's left to be done into sections. The one I'm standing in is where I'm spending my time this week."

"I don't want to be pushy, but can you use some help?" A pair of work gloves appeared in his hands from his back pocket. He held them up. "I can give you an hour or two. If I reach the trim and anything else that might be of use to me, we can negotiate."

What would Jeff say? Jeff wasn't there. She rubbed her lips. If Ian was going to help, she'd prefer he help her work on the section she'd already chosen. "Well, if you'll help me here. I don't know what else you're looking for, but this section is the one I want to clear away by the next sale."

"Which is when?"

She raised her eyebrows. "With your help, maybe this weekend."

"Kind of late to advertise it, though." He pulled on the gloves.

"Aw, around here people read all the posted pieces of paper in grocery stores and signs stuck up around the streets and a few local sites online. So, you want to help me on this side?"

"No problem, ma'am." His smile traveled to his eyes.

Ma'am? Aurora picked up a plastic bag with a brown paper sack inside, full of bolts and nuts with a few screws, tacks, and small nails thrown in. "I thought Mr. Hartley had bought all the little bits last Saturday. He took away two large jars."

"You don't understand old scavengers like your grandfather. They never leave a bit behind no matter how small. Although if it's bent out of shape, that's another story." He peered into a wooden box, about the size of a plastic milk crate, fingering the contents.

Aurora busied herself with dusting off more wood-framed windows, sorting them by size and stacking them just inside the barn door. They'd sold many of them on Saturday to a woman who said she made art projects with them. Maybe she'd return, or another artist would. There existed several never-ending stacks of windows. Replacing them must have been a big thing. She stopped for a moment to brush the stale-smelling dust off her face and wipe her nose.

After they'd worked in silence for a while, Ian pulled out his cell. "Mind a little music?" He tuned to some jazz and set his phone on top of a two-by-four.

Aurora smiled and continued what she'd been doing.

"Hey," a female voice shouted. Monica stood in the entrance. She wasn't dressed like a respiratory therapist, but in black slacks and a red and black print blouse. "Hi Aurora. I saw Jeff's truck. I was going to help out, but if he's here—" Approaching Aurora, Monica stopped when she spotted Ian.

"Hey, Monica, why aren't you at the hospital?" Aurora took off her gloves and laid them aside with the rag she'd been using to dust the windows. "Glad to see you, though."

"Had a doc appointment, so I took the whole day off." Her eyes went back to Ian again. "Hi. I'm Monica." She approached him and held out her hand.

"I'm sorry. Monica this is Ian. He's redoing a house here in town.

Ian, this is my friend Monica who is a respiratory therapist at the hospital. She's new to town, too."

He pulled off a glove. "I stopped by to poke around and to help, also." He grinned at Monica as he put his glove back on and turned away.

Monica mouthed the words, "Is that who I think it is?" Covertly pointing at him.

Aurora said, "Let's go inside and get some iced tea and a snack. Ian, want something?"

"I have a bottle of water in the truck but wouldn't mind a glass of sweet tea." He wiped his forehead and went back to what he was doing.

Aurora took Monica by the arm and led her toward the house. "You sure you want to get those clothes dirty? They look nice."

"Well, maybe you can lend me an old T-shirt like yours. Is the puppy back there in the basket?"

Aurora nodded and called over her shoulder, "Ian, it's going to be a few minutes. I'm going to find Monica something grungy to wear."

Ian waved and continued digging through bits and pieces.

As soon as they entered the house, Monica said, "That's the guy y'all were talking about yesterday?"

"Um—yeah," Aurora said. She gathered three tall plastic glasses and filled them with ice. "Pretty hot, huh."

Monica's eyes flared. "Too bad I'm married."

"And you have a good one, too."

Monica grinned. "Yep. I'm not in the mood for a trade."

They both laughed. Aurora said, "If Jeff and I hadn't hooked up back in Houston, I might have been."

"You'd be competing with Sarah."

"Don't tell anyone I said that, especially Sarah." She poured tea over the ice and put the glasses on a tray, taking a swallow from one, the sweetness clearing away the dry, dusty taste in her mouth. "Sarah has been staking him out. I don't think she'd mind if I told you. She thinks he might be some kind of criminal." Aurora wasn't going to say Sarah thought he might be a murderer.

"You know, Aurora, I don't know you well since we haven't lived here long. I think you and Jeff came around the same time as us, but you're from here, right?"

"Yes. I was brought up by my grandparents. You've probably figured that out by now. This was their house. When my grandfather died, he left the house to me and my brother, Harold. Harry has no plans to ever move back here, and I didn't want to sell the house. So, we bought out Harry. With Jeff's job, he can live anywhere."

"How did y'all meet? His being in hospital sales and you being a teacher, you couldn't have come into contact with each other professionally."

"One night I was in the bookstore at the mall, one of my favorite places, drinking coffee and reading a book about divorce. I had a small stack of other divorce books on the table."

"So, you were married before."

Aurora frowned. "Yeah. I'll just tell you outright. My husband abandoned me."

"What?"

"He and my best friend from college ran off together."

"You hear about that kind of thing—"

"Well, it happened."

"I'm sorry."

"Oh, it's okay. Been awhile now. Anyway, once they had run off and settled together somewhere else, he filed for divorce and started calling and demanding I give him stuff from our house, so I decided to get a lawyer. And I thought I should bone up on what was going on with divorces these days. I thought I'd get some books about how to find a good lawyer and how to proceed, etcetera." She rolled her shoulders back and released a deep sigh. "Come on in the bedroom. I'll find you an old shirt to put on. I have some extra-large T-shirts. They'll cover some of your pants, as well as your blouse, so they won't get all dusty."

"Y'all didn't have any kids?" Monica trailed Aurora the short distance to the small primary bedroom.

Aurora shook her head. "Ralph didn't want any. He didn't tell me until after we were married. I loved him, so even though I wanted a child, I gave in to him and didn't have any."

"You were at the bookstore with the divorce books and met Jeff? That's kind of sweet."

"Oh, yeah, that's what you were asking about." Aurora laughed. "I lost track. I had this pile of books on divorce sitting on the table and this guy comes over and asks if I mind if he shares my table because all the others are taken. I looked. All the other tables were, in fact, taken. He introduced himself and put his hand out, and we shook hands, which I thought was kind of weird. I tried to ignore him and thumb through the books. He sat and drank his coffee. I thought he was really cute, but I wasn't in the market."

"I can imagine."

Aurora rummaged around in the bottom drawer of an old chest and pulled out a wrinkled T-shirt with a college emblem. "I know a lot of people jump right into other relationships as soon as they're divorced—if not before. But I had no desire to even look at another man."

"So ... Jeff changed your mind?"

Aurora held the shirt out to Monica. "Here, try this. He got me to talking about my situation. We ended up talking for a couple of hours. He was so nice, and Ralph had been such an jerk. Jeff asked me about my lawyer, but I hadn't hired one yet, so he recommended someone."

Monica stripped off her blouse and pulled the T-shirt over her head. Even though she was tall, the shirt fell past her hips.

"I took the name down and chose a couple of the books and excused myself and went to the register to check out. After I paid, he was waiting for me near the exit. He asked me if I'd like to have coffee with him sometime. Well, he was so nice. We made a date to have coffee a few days later. He was such a gentleman, held the door for me, and shook my hand when we said goodbye. Really, both when we shook hands when we met and when we parted, he gave my hand a gentle squeeze ... a little jolt traveled up my arm."

"Ohhhh." Monica grinned, showing her dimples.

"Yeah. I couldn't help myself. Before long, we were meeting for coffee, or a light dinner if he wasn't off at some hospital somewhere selling medical stuff. He always paid. He said, "The man always pays." I thought he was old-fashioned, but who was I to argue, especially on a teacher's salary. I'd been thinking of getting a second job, but I was working on some mystery stories. I'd sold a few short stories by then. I hated to give up."

"You wanted to write full time?" She sat on the edge of the bed and let Aurora talk.

Aurora nodded. "Anyway, I got a lawyer. Since Ralph had abandoned me, my lawyer convinced his lawyer we should negotiate a settlement. We went to mediation. Would you believe Ralph brought Shelly with him to the mediation? She had to stay in the waiting room, but still—even his own lawyer saw what an jerk he was."

"So, when your divorce was finalized, you and Jeff got married?"

"What? No. I didn't want to get married again. I put the money from the divorce into a savings account."

"Meanwhile, what was Jeff saying? Did he want to get married? Had he been married before? I hope you don't mind me asking these questions. I don't want to be too nosy."

Aurora shrugged. "Jeff said he'd been married for several years but found out she was running around on him. Eventually he got tired of her lying, and they split up. He said he wasn't shopping for a wife."

"So how did you end up married if neither of you wanted to be married?"

"Well, uh, even though I knew better, I slept with Jeff way too soon. I won't bore you with the details, but he wined and dined me."

"I get the picture."

"He was so much fun to be with and so considerate. We started going to some fun things in Houston like the opera and museums and went down to Galveston to Mardi Gras. He was very sympathetic when my grandfather became ill and looked like he was not going to make it."

"Sounds like he supported you when you really needed it. Emotionally, I mean."

"He did. He was so charming and sweet. He drove me out here when Granddad was in the hospital. He called me when we weren't together, checking on me."

"Okay, well, I'm getting antsy about the actual marriage."

Aurora turned away. "I got pregnant."

"Oh, poop!"

"We didn't plan it. We had a lot of discussions about what to do. I'd actually always wanted a baby. Wait, I didn't tell you this, in mediation Ralph told me he and Shelly were going to start a family. After he said all those years he didn't want kids ... anyway, I told Jeff I wanted to keep the baby, but he didn't have to have a relationship with it if he chose not to as long as he'd help out financially. I thought he'd be squeamish about the idea of a baby, but he said he did want it, and he'd be an active parent. He showed up one night with a bouquet of eighteen lovely white roses and a ring and proposed. A justice of the peace married us soon after." She beckoned at Monica to follow her back to the kitchen.

"But wait, you don't have any kids."

"I lost the baby." Aurora cleared her throat. She hadn't meant to get teary-eyed. She hadn't meant to even tell Monica about the baby, but somehow, she had.

"Oh, I'm so sorry."

"Then, my grandfather died." Aurora squared her shoulders. "So, anyway, those are stories for another day." She grabbed three protein bars from a box on the counter. "Let's get this tea out to Ian before the ice is totally melted."

Monica stopped at the back door. "I was wondering, Aurora.

Aren't you afraid to work in your barn by yourself? I mean, this guy Ian. After what Georgina told us—"

Aurora waved her down. "Ian? Naw. He's harmless. I think Sarah's just neurotic sometimes, but don't tell her I said that." She didn't tell Monica there was something about Ian she couldn't put her finger on, something didn't feel right. He didn't scare her, exactly, but he had an edge to him. She'd have to think on it more when she was around him and see if she could identify what it was.

CHAPTER
SIX

"I watched him again at the house he's renovating."

Sarah stood at Aurora's back door, holding the screen open with an elbow. Her purse hung down from one hand. A plastic grocery sack, with a bouquet of fall flowers sticking out the top, weighed down the other.

"He who?" Aurora had been in the middle of an important chapter—well, every chapter was important—when someone banged at the back of the house. "And hello. Are those flowers for me?"

"HM," Sarah said. "They were on sale, so I bought us both a bouquet. The woman said the flowers weren't moving like they'd expected them to. And I brought us take out." Her eyes roved over Aurora's face. "Did you forget you invited me over for tonight? We're going to stream a movie?"

Aurora clapped a hand over her mouth. "Completely and totally forgot."

"That says a lot about our friendship. But let me in, the wind is blowing me to pieces."

Aurora backed away from the door so Sarah could swoop inside and plow into the kitchen, dumping the bag and her purse and keys onto the counter. "Whew. My arms were getting tired." She looked under the sink and found a vase for the flowers.

Aurora followed her. "Who are you talking about? Ian?"

"Yeah, Ian, the Handsome Man. Did you forget that's my name for him? I drove over there after school today. I saw Jeff's truck, only of course, it wasn't Jeff's. Ian was hanging off the front porch of his old house, hammering some trim into place. I sailed on by. I don't think he saw me." She took an aluminum container out of the bag and pulled the cardboard cover off, revealing spaghetti stuffed inside. Garlic and tomato sauce aromas filled the air. A smaller bag, a paper one, held four large pieces of garlic bread. Another container held salad and a mini-Styrofoam cup filled with Italian dressing.

Aurora's mouth watered. "Did we talk about you bringing dinner? I don't remember that, either." She leaned her face over the spaghetti and breathed in the steam. "I'm not saying you shouldn't have brought it. I just don't remember."

Sarah glanced at the ceiling and shook her head. "It's my fault. I called you in the morning when you were working on your book."

"Like now."

"Oh. I'm sorry. Do I keep catching you in the middle of an important scene or something? I don't mean to. Anyway, let me get the bottle of wine out of my car, and then I'll set the table while you finish what you were doing, and we can have dinner, and then maybe you can go back with me, and I'll show you where he lives." She drew a deep breath.

"Wine, too? How much do I owe you?"

Sarah had headed out the door and said, over her shoulder, "Nothing. You can get it next time. Go finish up."

Aurora wished Sarah knew *finishing up* wasn't so easy, but she didn't say anything. She'd just end the sentence she'd been in the middle of and shut down the computer. The puppy needed feeding anyway. Poor little thing hadn't made much progress other than drinking and pooping. That's all they could ask for now. She placed the puppy in the basket and took her into the kitchen. After very little coaxing, the puppy latched onto the tiny bottle. A couple of minutes later, the pup had her fill.

Sarah had returned and gone to the drawer in the kitchen where she knew Aurora kept the corkscrew. "This is one of my favs. They don't always have it in stock." After opening the bottle, she took two glasses out of the cabinet and poured red wine into each of them. Handing one to Aurora, she said, "Here's to future possibilities."

Sarah should've let the wine rest for a few minutes, but since she hadn't, Aurora put her nose into the glass and inhaled the pleasant bouquet. She sipped and watched her friend over the top of her wine glass. Sarah had some kind of plan. Aurora didn't know what it was, but Sarah always had a plan.

"Good, huh?" Sarah raised her eyebrows. "So will you go with me?"

"To see Ian's house? Why? What are you up to?" She put down the glass and ran warm water over her hands at the sink.

Sarah picked up the bottle and led the way to the table in the little dining room. "To see if he's attached. To see if anyone—a woman, though I guess it could be a man—shows up at his house this evening. If he's living with someone—or even dating someone—he's probably not the serial killer."

"I don't think that's true from what I've read. But, anyway, you're really looking for a hook-up, right?" Aurora set the basket down next to her chair and sat down at the head of the table, which was usually Jeff's place.

Sarah began dishing out the spaghetti. She dropped a huge meatball in the middle of a plate and set it in front of Aurora. "You need your protein."

Not sure why Sarah thought so, Aurora shrugged. She laid garlic bread on each plate and put some salad on small plates. "Okay, sit down, and tell me what you're up to, without being crude."

Sarah set her own plate down and poured more wine in each

glass. "You mean you don't want me to say I want to get into Ian's pants?"

"Ugh. Exactly." She forked a bite of meatball into her mouth. Once she'd swallowed, she said, "Good."

"I mean, only if I decide he's not the killer."

"First of all, you're being silly. Secondly, you have no evidence."

"He did give me the evil eye when I said what I said on Saturday."

"I would have too, by the way."

After downing a mouthful of food, Sarah said, "If he's not and doesn't have anyone, I don't see why I shouldn't get in the running. And the only way I'll know if he does have someone is if I observe him."

"You mean you'll stalk him and find out which he is, the killer or the potential love interest?"

"I teach all day. How could I stalk him?"

"In the evenings, like you're planning for tonight."

"I just want to casually drive by and, if he's outside, ask him if he needs anything, offer to help make his stay here as pleasant as possible."

Aurora gave her an *I-understand-what-you'd-really-be-offering* look. "You could have talked to him if you'd been here. He stopped by and helped me sort through the stuff in the barn."

Sarah slapped the table. "Why didn't you call me?"

"Because, as you said, you're a teacher and have to teach. It was in mid-afternoon."

"How was he?"

"Helpful. He identified a few things he could use, so I sold them to him."

"Without asking Jeff?"

"Jeff doesn't need to know. Besides, this is my inheritance, not his. I can do with it what I want."

For a moment, Sarah focused on twirling the spaghetti around her fork, then she raised skeptical eyes to Aurora.

"I can," Aurora said. "I can, and I did."

"Jeff did put up some of the money to buy your brother out."

"Yeah. But I did it anyway and unless someone says something, he'll never know."

"Aren't you worried about Ian being here when Jeff is out of town? I mean, people talk. What would Jeff say if he found out?"

"Why would he say anything?" She wondered what Sarah was getting at.

"Jeff doesn't strike me as being secure."

"Oh, he's just adjusting to everything, especially moving to a new town where he doesn't know anyone. He'll be okay. Everything takes time. I'm the one who should be having problems, depressed even."

Sarah picked at her salad, stabbing a large mouthful. She chewed, swallowed, sipped her wine, stared at her plate some more. "I'm sorry. I'm always putting my foot in my mouth. This time both feet."

"I'll be okay, Sarah. Jeff wants us to try again. I'm not ready yet." She didn't know when she would be if what she suspected about Jeff turned out to be true.

"And you're not sure what he's up to."

Aurora shrugged. Sarah had known her long enough to practically read her mind. "Yeah. In the meantime, I'm hoping we'll at least get a dog."

Sarah laughed. "Some substitute. Are you thinking of keeping the little one who's in the basket next to your chair?"

"Maybe. We'll see." She didn't want to say she was thinking of getting a *big* dog. Sarah would want an explanation, one Aurora wasn't ready to give. She hadn't told anyone about the light in the barn. She didn't want to worry anyone. "Anyway, I wish you'd give Jeff a break. On a scale of one to a hundred, losing a baby and moving to a new town are way off the scale."

"Listen to you. One minute you're suspecting he's having an

affair. Then you're talking about having a baby in the future. And now you're defending him."

Aurora put her face in her hands. "I'm so conflicted. What if I'm just imagining things? Maybe I didn't smell perfume? Maybe I'm insecure because of what Ralph did. I could subconsciously be looking for the same behavior in Jeff." She raised her head and rubbed her eyes. "I'm glad we moved here. It's good for me, if not for him. I have lots of good memories of growing up here. I have you and other friends. The move wasn't traumatic for me at all."

"But the baby."

"I'm working through it. I saw a therapist, though Jeff wouldn't go with me. Can we change the subject now?"

"Jeff's such a typical man. He fits the stereotype—at least the one in my mind. Anyway, changing the subject back to Ian . . ."

"Monica stopped by and helped for a while, too. If anyone wanted to make anything out of Ian being here—even if he never came inside—"

"Monica was here? Didn't you just say it was mid-afternoon? Why wasn't she at work? Did she flirt with him?"

"Yes. Yes. She had a doctor's appointment. And no, if you had Tommy at home, would you spend your time flirting with Ian?"

"I guess not. Tommy is a hunk. So, she helped you. That was nice of her."

"She worked for about an hour before having to go pick up Ava from school. She'd promised Ava if the doctor's appointment didn't take all afternoon, they could go to the library. Ava always finishes her books way before they're due, so they were headed to get more."

"Monica's a good mother." Sarah's face held a wistful expression. She cleared her throat and slurped some wine in an effort to bring humor into the conversation.

"So, are you thinking of Ian as husband material? Because from what he's said, he loves to travel around the country with Gerhard."

"Oh yeah, the dog, but Ian could be getting lonely for some female companionship."

"Maybe he's gay."

"I hope not. Why are so many good-looking guys gay?"

"I had a hairdresser once who was gay. He said, 'Why are so many good-looking guys straight?'"

"Well, there's only one way to find out. Will you go with me?"

Aurora pushed back from the table. "Let me take care of this baby for a minute. I'll be right back." The puppy needed to be cleaned up after wetting the toweling under her, so Aurora took her back to the little pallet she'd made for her in a cardboard box. She wiped her off and dried her and put her down next to the desk. The pup had yet to even stand up for more than a moment, so Aurora wasn't worried about leaving her alone. She washed her hands again and went back to the table. "Now, where were we?"

Sarah had poured each of them more wine. "I was asking whether you'd take a ride with me past Ian's house, and if he's there, stop and visit."

"Do I have a choice?" Aurora bit into the remainder of the meatball. "Don't give me any more wine," she said with her mouth full.

"You always have a choice, but I *am* your best friend. I don't ask for much."

Aurora squeezed her eyes shut and shook her head. Sarah wasn't going to quit until Aurora agreed to go with her. Besides, what would it hurt? "Okay. But it's getting dark. What do you expect to see in the dark?"

"At least whether he has company for the evening."

"A drive-by won't give you an answer. His company could be coming later."

"If we park around the corner from his house, we can still see the front, so we'll be able to see if anyone is already there. Then if not, if we stay a little while, we'll see if anyone comes by."

Aurora's eyebrows shot up. "Doing a stake-out is different from stalking?"

"Can we use your car? He knows y'all's work truck, but he probably doesn't know your car, right?"

"He could. I park on the street like most everyone else around here. My car was on the street yesterday. The work truck was in the driveway."

"But your neighbors park on the street, too, right?"

"Not the one across the street. I only ever see an SUV pulled up in the yard. But, yeah, sometimes they or their company does. And sometimes people park in front of our house and go down to the bayou."

"We could take mine, I guess. I don't think he noticed me driving by."

"How many times have you driven by?"

Sarah did an eye roll.

"You don't even know, do you? God. You must be desperate."

"Can you be ready in the next few minutes before the sun has totally gone down?"

Aurora nodded. She hurried and finished her spaghetti and salad. After washing up, Aurora wrapped the puppy in a baby blanket and grabbed her purse and keys. "All ready."

"I'll help you clean up the kitchen when we get back."

"No problem. Let's go. We'll take my car. You can hold the puppy and direct me."

The sky had started turning oranges, purples, and blues. Only a few clouds hung around. The moon had shown its face. With the breeze, it was chilly but not uncomfortable. Sarah directed Aurora to the house, which was only a few miles East, in town but not in the middle of town. When they turned onto the street where Ian's house was located, the porch light was on. A light shone from the back of the house, too, but the rest of the house was dark. Ian's truck was gone.

"What do you want to do?" Aurora drove around the corner to where Sarah had designated a good place to surveil Ian's house, made a U-turn, and parked. She cracked a window to let a little breeze in. "Are you thinking we'd wait a while to see if and when he returns?"

The puppy whimpered. Sarah stroked the pup's downy head. "He was there earlier."

"He could have gone out to eat or to the store."

"You mind waiting just a little while?"

"Just a little while." Aurora adjusted the drivers' seat all the way back and stretched her legs. "Want me to take the baby?"

Sarah shook her head. "We're all right."

When Ian hadn't shown up after forty-five minutes, Aurora gave Sarah a look she was sure Sarah could see even in the dark. The moon, being a quarter, provided little light. They both glanced at the house.

Sarah sighed a deep, long sigh. Aurora yawned. They looked at each other again.

"He could be over at a girlfriend's house. Or a potential girl-friend's house." Aurora chewed on her bottom lip. She hated to burst Sarah's bubble. She wouldn't tell her Ian hadn't appeared interested in her last Saturday. He hadn't followed her with his eyes when she left their conversation. He hadn't watched her during the time he'd been at the sale. All those things would surely have indicated some interest. Sarah had been blind to them, though, because she'd gotten it in her head, she and Ian could be an item.

"You're right," Sarah said. "If he was out to eat alone, he'd be home by now. If he'd been at the grocery store, he'd be home by now. If he's at dinner with another woman, he won't be home for a while. Let's go."

"I'm sorry," Aurora said and started the car. "Maybe another day? I just want to say one thing, though, Sarah. I wasn't going to mention it, but I have to tell you how I feel."

"Which is what?"

Aurora pulled away from the curb. "I have this feeling about him. I mean, he's cute and all, but something just feels off. You know what I mean? Something about him just doesn't ring true."

"You think he could be the killer, too?"

"I wouldn't go as far as to say that ..."

"And yet you're not afraid of being home alone with him?"

"I can't put my finger on it. I didn't feel threatened the other day, just ..." Aurora shrugged.

Sarah grunted and crossed her arms. "Well, I know what I'm going to do when I get home. I'm going to google him."

CHAPTER
SEVEN

A car door slammed nearby, prompting Aurora to step out of the deep interior of the barn. She'd worked all morning on her novel, accomplishing the goal she'd set out for the day. After a quick lunch, she grabbed the basket, set the puppy inside, and headed out to get more of the never-ending pile of Grandfather's junk sorted, having definitely decided to hold another sale on Saturday. If she could get enough done, she could spend Friday getting ready for the sale.

Now, across the street, a uniformed man had stepped out of a constable's SUV. He glanced up and down the street. Spotting Aurora, he nodded. She nodded. He circled the car and climbed the steps to the house across the street. Aurora went back to the interior of the barn and stayed just inside where she could see what was going on.

The house's front door faced the bayou, so Aurora couldn't see if anyone came to the door. After a couple of minutes, she went back to work. Moments later, the rising and falling blast from a siren in the distance grew closer and closer. Aurora stepped back outside. A police car with flashing lights pulled to the curb behind the constable's car. A few minutes later, another siren, a bit different, sounded. Aurora stood fixed in place until a sheriff's SUV pulled in front of her house and parked. A uniformed woman climbed out of the police car. A male deputy exited the sheriff's car. Both jogged up the stairs of the house across the street.

Aurora's mystery writer's mind immediately concluded someone was horribly injured, or dead. Aurora and Jeff had never met the neighbor or neighbors. With every property being over-sized, some being as much as three-quarters of an acre or even more, they didn't often see many people. No one had come to greet them with a plate of freshly-baked cookies, or any other welcome gift when they'd moved in. She'd only seen a small, silver-gray SUV parked in the yard a couple of times. She'd always figured she'd go meet the neighbors if she and they were ever outside at the same time. So far, that hadn't happened.

Aurora brushed at her clothes and pulled off her gloves. She strode to the edge of her unfenced yard. Cupping her hand above her eyes to shield them from the sun, she stood adjacent to the sheriff's car and watched. A third siren wailed in the distance, and, before long, an ambulance pulled up followed by a fire truck. Two young people, a man and a woman, also climbed the stairs. Three firefighters jumped out of their truck and stood around talking to each other.

Whatever was going on couldn't be good. The house had no real porch, only a stoop, so when a person reached the top of the stairs, they had about a five-foot platform to stand on, with a wooden railing, and a short overhang. Someone must have somehow gained access to the house, because one of the uniformed men exited the house, followed by another, and spoke to each other before zeroing in on Aurora across the street.

After exchanging a few more words between them, a police officer approached the firefighters and conferred with them for a few moments. The men, and one woman, frowned and nodded. One of them spoke into a radio before the three of them scrambled back into the fire truck. The driver started it up. After they left, the police officer jogged across to Aurora.

Stomach in a flutter, she swallowed and reminded herself she hadn't done anything wrong. Like most people she knew, though, being approached by a police officer, or being stopped in her car by a police officer, caused her knees to weaken.

"Ma'am," he said, "I'm Officer Quincy Dalton. Is this your residence?" He inclined his head toward her house. Dalton appeared to be about the same age as Aurora but towered over her five three-and-a-half. He had light brown hair and bulging muscular shoulders in a short-sleeved uniform shirt. Dark glasses concealed his eyes. A faint scent of manly sweat accompanied him.

"Yes. What's going on over there?" Aurora squinted at him in the sunlight.

"Do you mind giving me your name?"

"Not at all. Aurora Morris." She looked down at her attire, realizing she looked like a thrift store reject again in her work boots, old jeans, and another stained T-shirt. She shifted her gloves to her left hand and held out her right to shake his.

He shook her hand with his callused warm one and asked, "Do you mind if I ask you a few questions?"

"I'll answer them, if I can. But can we go sit on my front porch in the shade? I've been working in my barn, and I could use a break from standing."

"Sure thing," he said, turning and giving the officer across the street a thumbs up.

She and Jeff had kept her grandparents' old wooden rockers for the time being. She led the way across the yard and up the three steps, sitting on the rocking chair closest to the bayou and indicating he should sit in the other. "Need anything?"

"No, ma'am. I'm good. If you don't mind, just a few questions. How long have you lived here?"

"Just a few months."

"Didn't an old couple own this house? I've patrolled this neighborhood and seemed like I saw an elderly man and woman coming and going over the years."

"My grandparents. The Ivys. My grandmother died not too long ago and then my grandfather recently."

He nodded. "You inherited the house then?"

"My brother and I did, yes. They raised us when our parents died. My husband and I bought out my brother and moved here intending to modernize the house—bring it up to date. Right now, we're clearing out the old building back there. The barn, I call it."

"Your husband's name is?"

"Jeff Morris. Jeffery."

"Is he home today?"

"He's in sales and often travels. He's out of town this week."

"Okay. Well, what I'm—we're—wondering is whether you knew the person who lived across the street."

Aurora shook her head, noting he used the past tense. "No. I used to when we were kids. There was a little family. But since we moved here, I never even saw who lived there. I knew someone did, because an SUV came and went sometimes, but that's all."

"You never saw anyone? Not who lived there or any visitors or anybody?"

"I never even saw the mail carrier stop to deliver mail. No one. Like I said, only the car indicated someone lived there, or at least spent some time there." She spread her arms. "With these streets being as wide as they are, sounds from across the way or across the bayou don't carry like they do when houses are closer. I'd have to be really looking to notice someone. Did something happen to whoever it was?"

He peeled off his sunglasses, revealing eyes the color of a much-handled penny, with glints of copper. His eyes roved over her face as if judging whether her responses had been genuine. Aurora recognized his expression for what it was. She had often looked at some of her students with the same scrutiny.

"Was someone living there when you and your husband moved in? Or did they move in after y'all did?"

"I have no idea. I don't remember seeing a vehicle when I'd visit my grandfather, but someone could have lived there. If my grandfather was still alive, he'd be able to tell you everything you want to know. He made it his business to know everyone and everything in this neighborhood."

"Do you work, ma'am? I mean, do you ever work outside the home?"

"I'm a writer. I write mysteries." Though she hadn't published a book yet, Aurora still called herself a writer. She'd had, at least, a few stories published.

He nodded. "Yeah? I read thrillers and mystery books."

"Probably not the kind I write. I'm working on a mystery right now with a female point of view." She wasn't going to tell him she was thinking of having a serial killer in her novel. She wasn't sure if she would. She still needed to do some research. "I don't think many men read mysteries with a female lead character."

"Oh. Women's books."

She forced a laugh. "Yes. Do you mind telling me what happened over there? I mean, I know enough to know cops aren't supposed to tell people what they're doing, right?"

"I can't share anything with you at this stage."

"Let me ask you this, do you think I should be worried? Could I be in any danger? I'm often here by myself." She wasn't going to tell him about the light in the barn and all, either. It would just complicate matters and couldn't have anything to do with whatever happened across the street.

He studied her for a few moments. "I can't answer you. Right now, no one is sure what happened exactly."

"But someone is dead over there, or y'all—the constable, the police, the sheriff, and an ambulance—wouldn't be here, right?"

"Okay, yes. Someone is dead. That's all I know."

She swallowed the taste of fear in her mouth. "Can you tell me if it was natural causes or . . . uh . . ."

"Not sure at this point."

"Well, was it a woman or a man?" Her stomach twisted in exasperation.

He stood and shook his head.

She stood and shook her head, unintentionally mimicking him. "What should I do? Do I need to protect myself?"

"Keep your doors locked, but you should always keep your doors locked these days. Do you have a dog?"

"If I had a dog, he would have been barking his head off." The puppy didn't count.

"What about a gun? I don't recommend it, but this is Texas. You probably have a gun, right?"

She shook her head again. "Guns scare me."

"Well, ma'am, I don't know what to tell you."

"At some point in the future will I be able to find out what went on over there? For my own protection?"

"Probably. Something might be in the paper next week."

"Next week!" The newspaper for their little town was a weekly, coming out every Wednesday. Since the day was Thursday, Aurora didn't want to wait a week to find out more information. She doubted the Houston Chronicle would carry the news of something like this happening in a suburb. Frowning, she forced herself to refrain from showing her disgust. "Well, then, I guess I'll have to wait and hope I'll be okay for the time being."

"Yes, ma'am. Do you mind if I come back if I have any more questions?" He slipped his glasses back on.

"No, officer." She stopped herself from giving him the stink eye. "But I don't know what else I'd be able to tell you."

He jogged back across the yard and the street and up the steps.

Aurora walked back to the barn and stood right inside the entrance. She knew what she had to do even if she had to wait all day. Taking her cell phone from an old side table on which it lay, she texted Georgina. *"Pls call me asap. I need you to find out something for me. Can't say in a text. Tks."*

Often, she was frustrated. Most of her friends worked outside the home and couldn't hold lengthy conversations. Thank goodness for texts. At least she could set up the call. She couldn't wait a week to find out the details of the dead person.

While she worked, she kept an eye on the activity at the house across the street. Eventually, another vehicle came. The driver wore a suit, and authority emanated from him like an aura. The constable left soon after. The next time she looked, the sheriff's car was gone, leaving police, ambulance, and the suit. By chance, she was outside dumping trash into their work truck when two people came out with what had to be a covered body on a stretcher, which they loaded into the ambulance. They departed, sans siren.

Aurora wanted to cross the street and demand they tell her what happened. She knew they wouldn't, but darn, shouldn't neighbors be informed so they could be on guard? She still stood next to the work truck when one of the police officers retrieved crime scene tape from their cruiser. The suit left. The two police officers stretched crime scene tape from stair rail to stair rail. Officer Dalton's eyes met hers. He didn't smile. He said something to the other officer. They left.

Aurora considered crossing over and looking in the windows. She texted Sarah, knowing there would be no response until after school dismissed for the day. *Have news! Pls come to my house after dark. Bring a flashlight. I'll explain later."*

CHAPTER
EIGHT

Thursday evening, Aurora was in the zone, racing through a new chapter, excited at the progress she'd made. She'd showered and changed into a pair of tie-dyed sweatpants and a faded, long-sleeved shirt she'd been given when she'd completed a five-K walk several years earlier. She'd talked with Georgina who had agreed to let her know as soon as she heard any details involving the neighbor. Now, even though she was somewhat creeped out at being home alone, she'd kind of been inspired with ideas spinning in her head.

"What is that?"

The down on Aurora's neck stood on end before her brain registered the speaker was Jeff. Anyone who knew Jeff would have recognized his tone of voice, but Aurora was already on edge. When she turned, he was staring at the puppy in the basket on the floor. "I didn't hear you come in. Why didn't you call and let me know you'd be home a day early?" Standing, she slipped her arms around his neck, giving him a hug followed by a sloppy kiss. "I didn't think you were coming home until tomorrow."

He responded with a firm squeeze. "What's the furry thing in the basket?"

He wore jeans and a long-sleeved, plaid button-up shirt, the collar half turned under. He smelled woody and fresh, like he'd just stepped out of the shower and splashed on some cologne. Could he have come home and she didn't even notice? Talk about being in the zone. She straightened his collar before answering him.

"A rescue puppy. Isn't she sweet? You can't see much unless you hold her." Aurora scooped up the puppy and placed her in Jeff's hands.

"We said we were going to discuss it—getting a dog." He stroked the pup's head and finally a smile turned up the edges of his mouth, though it did look a bit forced.

"I know. We are. Taylor just asked me to foster this baby until they could find a home. She won't be here forever." Aurora would like to have the puppy forever. She had grown attached to the pup already. She had also thought more about having a big dog. She'd broach getting any kind of dog later.

Jeff cupped the puppy and examined her closer. "She's soft."

"Why are you here? Wait, I meant, *Wow*, glad you're home a day early, but what's up?" Aurora had this thing about not wanting anyone to read her writing, at least until she'd edited it a bit, so she closed her laptop.

Still cuddling the pup, he shrugged at the same time his stomach growled. "Finished earlier than I thought. Do we have anything in the house to eat?"

Aurora didn't usually fix dinner when he was gone. He usually ate on the road. "There's leftover spaghetti Sarah brought the other day from Parmesan's. I could fix a salad to go with it."

"Sounds good."

"Let me get you a beer, and we can talk while I get supper ready."

"Thanks." He kissed her cheek. "This little thing is not any bigger than a stuffed toy." He laid the pup back in the basket before taking Aurora's hand and leading her to the kitchen. "Have you eaten?"

"I had a late lunch. A huge salad. I'll sit with you while you eat, though." She had a lot to tell him but hadn't decided how much she wanted to share.

Jeff took down a plate and utensils and sat at the kitchen table where he could watch her.

She pulled the leftovers and a beer out of the refrigerator, handing the beer to him and filling his plate with spaghetti.

"Is something bothering you? You want to talk about it? You looked startled when I came in." Jeff popped the top on the beer can and took a long swallow, his eyes not leaving her face.

Aurora slid the covered plate into the microwave and turned to look at him. "There was some excitement in our neighborhood." She laid a napkin and placemat in front of him before she leaned against the counter, arms crossed. "I've been a little on edge since this afternoon." Just thinking about all the commotion across the street caused her fingers to tingle.

"What happened? You're not hurt or anything, are you? You look okay."

"I was working in the barn when I heard some noise and, uh, first one cop car came, then another, then a bunch of police and an ambulance and a fire truck. They parked in front of the house across the street and went in."

"We've never met whoever lives there, have we? I don't remember. I guess someone could have come to our sale. There were a lot of people."

When the microwave beeped, Aurora stirred the food and put it back in for another minute. "No. I don't know who lived there. Past tense. After a long time, the ambulance took someone away."

Jeff's face blanched. "Lived? Someone died over there?"

"They must have. I mean, yeah. The EMTs carried out a stretcher with a body on it."

Neither of them spoke for a minute until the microwave bell rang. Aurora gave him the plate. "I'll be right back." She went to her desk and retrieved her phone, taking it to the bathroom. *Sarah, don't come tonite. Jeff's home. TTYL.* She turned off her phone and slipped it into her pocket. After flushing the commode, she returned to the table and sat down adjacent to her husband.

Jeff forked spaghetti into his mouth and swallowed. "Did you talk to the police? Did they tell you what happened?"

"I tried, but all they would do was take down our names since I didn't know anything. I wish now I had at least met the person."

"Yeah. Maybe we ought to try to meet some of the other neighbors. I'd feel better about leaving you alone here when I'm out of town."

"I've been thinking I'd like to know some of them, too." She hesitated and sipped her wine, rolling it around on her tongue. "I might as well tell you. I didn't want to worry you since it wasn't a big thing."

He put down his fork and took a sip of beer. "What is it? Did something else happen?"

"Kind of." She watched his face, hoping he wouldn't get angry when she told him what had happened the week before. "Last Thursday—a week ago tonight ..." She wasn't sure how she should tell him."

"Well, what?"

Blurting the story out might be the best bet. "Someone was in the barn in the middle of the night."

"Last Thursday night, before I got home ... Well, of course it had to be before I got home." He grasped the edge of the table. "What time was this?"

"Okay, well, the middle of the night." Rising and going back to the counter, Aurora refilled her wine glass and took another sip of the tart red. She leaned against the counter again. "I woke up from a bad dream and had to pee. I went into the bathroom and when I did, a light shone in the window. Not real bright. Not like someone was right outside the house shining a light through the window. It was distant."

"Are you sure you didn't dream it? You could have."

74

"What? No. I know. I got up to pee," she said again.

"Okay, but when you wake up, sometimes you're so groggy you imagine things. I don't mean you specifically, but people do. They think they see things or hear things."

What was he talking about? "I was groggy, yes, but a light came in the window."

"Couldn't it have been a car passing by on the other side of the vacant lot?"

"Jeff, you're not listening to me." She gritted her teeth. "A light came from the direction of the barn."

"How did you know it came from the barn?"

"I didn't at first. I stepped into the bathtub and looked out the window, and the light flashed from the direction of the barn." She flinched as she remembered being surprised and feeling jittery.

"From the direction. You mean from inside the barn?"

"Yes. From inside." She clenched her fists. She wanted him to believe her, not to doubt her.

The muscles around Jeff's mouth tightened. "Oh, honey, I bet you were scared stiff." He stood and took her in his arms.

She let him pull her close. His strong arms and warm body made her feel safe and secure. "Honestly, I wasn't afraid, at first. I thought probably some kids were in the barn."

"I'm sorry you had to go through that. Did you have trouble going back to sleep? I bet you did."

Rearing back and looking him in the face, Aurora said, "Uh, I ..."

"Tell me you didn't go out there." He peered into her face.

"I did. I put on my robe and shoes and turned on the flashlight on my phone. The light flashed every now and again. I was kind of angry at the idea someone would be trying to steal some of our junk, especially when we were going to sell it so cheap."

He shook his head. "How could you be so stupid?" He sat back down and patted the chair next to him. "Was it kids or what? I can't believe you went out there!"

Aurora dropped into the chair and took another swallow of her wine, finally feeling the warmth spread through her body. At least Jeff wasn't angry at her for being so stupid. He seemed more concerned. "I don't know who it was. When I got close, the person ran out and knocked me down, practically ran over me and out into the street and up the slope toward Main Street."

"So, you couldn't see who it was? Couldn't see if it was a man or a woman or a kid?"

She shook her head. "I don't think it was a woman. Probably a man, though it could have been a big kid. All I saw as they ran was a dark hoodie pulled up over their head."

"Why didn't you tell me before?" He laid his hand on her forearm.

"I was afraid you'd be mad."

"Never. You know I always worry about you when I'm out of town. We've talked about your being home alone and how to take precautions."

Aurora thought she remembered their discussion. "I'm sorry. Maybe I should have called the police, but I really thought it was probably kids. I can handle kids after teaching all those years. I was just going to yell at them. Turned out to be only one person. And I wasn't hurt. In fact, I wasn't really scared after a few minutes. I dusted myself off and went back to bed." She wasn't really scared. She'd been shaking and had watery knees, but she didn't want him to know.

He shook his head. "Next time—I hope there's not a next time— but if something happens again, *never* go outside. *Never* confront them. Okay? Promise me?"

Grateful his response was so mild, Aurora nodded. "I want to ask you something, and I hope you'll say yes."

"Okay, what?" He cocked his head. "You know I hardly ever tell you no."

She hesitated. She wasn't so sure about that. "Well, after the barn thing, and whatever happened across the street, I want to get a dog. A big dog. A barker."

Jeff laughed. "I know we said we were going to discuss it further, but I don't think that's going to be necessary. As far as I'm concerned, on Monday when you're volunteering, you can pick out the best dog they have. Whichever one Taylor recommends."

Aurora leaped up and planted herself on his lap. She gave him a big kiss and wrapped her arms around him, rocking him back and forth and laughing.

Jeff hugged her back. "Just be sure he's housebroken, okay?"

"Okay, I will. Thank you so much. Do you care what kind of dog?"

"No. A dog dog." He grinned. "They often make the best pets."

"This will make Taylor happy. They have way too many animals at the shelter." She went back to her chair.

"And while I'm thinking about it. I only casually looked at the windows and door locks when we moved in," Jeff said. "This weekend I'll check them all and go to the hardware store for sturdy replacements. That'll be my weekend project."

"In addition to another sale."

His expression was deadpan. "Okay. In addition to another sale. I noticed the truck was loaded with stuff. You must have gotten a lot done in the barn."

No way she was going to tell him about Ian stopping by. "Some. I think if we work in there tomorrow, we can have plenty of stuff to sell on Saturday. I told the folks I talked to last Saturday we hoped to have a sale every week and to look for the flyers around town."

"Have you already put the flyers up?"

"Not yet. I wanted to wait and see how far I could get. Now, with you here, it'll be worth our time and the buyers' time to go ahead and open up. But what do you think of limiting it in the morning from seven to twelve?"

"Good for me. We can have most of the weekend to ourselves."

"I was thinking we could set those hours from now on. We don't want to be a slave to this house—any more than we already are."

"Are you sorry we took this on?" He raised his eyebrows.

"I'm not. Are you? I love it here. I just worry about you."

He glanced away and then took another bite of his food.

Aurora said, "Are you regretting this? I mean, I know it's been hard on you, traveling during the week and working on the house on weekends."

"You're the one I've been wondering about." He laid his hand on hers.

Their eyes met. "You mean losing the baby. That's different. Anyway, I'll be all right. My writing is distracting. I have so many ideas. And it's good connecting with my friends again."

"I just want you to be happy. I don't want you to have any regrets about moving here—about marrying me, in fact." He squeezed her hand.

Her thoughts went to their whirlwind romance. They'd had so much fun together. Then came her grandfather passing away and dealing with the house and all. "It has been hard some days, but those times are rarer and rarer. I'm glad we're here, that we've started the rest of our lives out here where life is not as hectic."

"Yeah, even though something happened to whoever lived across the street." He grimaced. "By the way, not to be morbid, but did you call the attorney about the deed—deeds—and our wills? Oh, and the insurance agent?"

She'd been dragging her feet on getting the property put in both their names in equal shares. Since she'd been divorced once, in the back of her mind was the thought that if she and Jeff were to divorce, he'd be entitled to half the house even though the part of the money he'd put forward to buy out Harry's share wasn't anywhere near half. "Not yet."

"Honey, you agreed to put the house in both names. If we're both going to put our sweat into it, that's only fair. And, you know, I'll be putting more physical labor into this place than you will. Sweat equity." He grinned.

"I know. I know. But I thought once we obtained the mortgage after the remodeling, we'd put the house in both names then."

"What about our wills?"

She shook her head. "No. We do need wills. I sure don't want my ex to get any of my stuff. I don't know the law, but he'd try, anyway. Everything has to go to you. I promise I'll call the lawyer first thing."

"Good. Come here." He took her hand and dragged her toward him. "It's probably not important to you, but I'd feel a lot better knowing everything is taken care of." He stroked her cheek.

"I realize that. Once we get our wills done, if something happens to me, you'll get the whole house, and vice versa. I swear I'll do it tomorrow while you're out buying hardware to secure the windows and doors." She laughed and let herself be pulled onto his lap. More than a few days had passed since they'd been physically close. She knew what he wanted, and she wanted it, too.

"We're partners in everything, right?" He kissed her and led her into the bedroom, slowing only to start peeling off her clothing.

Aurora wasn't really in the mood to make love but gave in as she usually did. She didn't want her husband to be one of those who looked elsewhere for intimacy. She held out hope he wasn't already.

Afterward, as she lay encircled in Jeff's arms, Aurora pushed all her concerns away. *Maybe he wasn't having an affair. Maybe she was mistaken. Maybe the perfume smell was from some woman at a hospital. She could only hope so. She couldn't tolerate a cheating husband a second time.*

When Jeff had fallen asleep, she tended to the puppy, holding her close and stroking her soft, little body. Aurora didn't know why she'd been hesitating about the legal paperwork on the house. Jeff loved her. He'd proven that since they'd been married. Maybe it was the idea she would no longer have anything wholly and completely hers. Jeff was adamant she make the house joint property. And they needed to have life insurance on each other. And their wills should leave everything to each other. When she climbed back into bed and drifted off, Aurora slept feeling confident Jeff, unlike her first husband, had no intention of going anywhere.

CHAPTER
NINE

First thing Aurora did, after cooking breakfast, straightening up the kitchen, and making the bed, was call an attorney, as promised. She'd liked the one who'd handled both her grandfather's estate and the issue regarding buying out her brother's interest in the house. He'd be perfect to address the two things still needing to be done. She didn't tell Jeff. She'd surprise him the next time he asked. The receptionist, who greeted Aurora like she was an old friend, said as soon as the lawyer returned from court, she'd give him the message.

When Aurora joined Jeff in the barn, his stance was rigid, and he waved his arm across the interior. "What have you been doing all week? When I saw the truck was so full, I thought you'd be further along than this."

Caught off guard, Aurora's stomach churned, reminding her she might need to make a doctor's appointment to see what could be done about the constant stomach issues. Speechless, she could only think getting laid hadn't left Jeff feeling as good as she'd thought it would. She'd accommodated him, even though she hadn't been in the mood, and now this. She wasn't sure how to respond. Every day she'd worked for several hours. She'd made a trip to the dump. She'd stacked stuff she thought he'd want to look at. Maybe he'd forgotten what the barn looked like the previous weekend.

"Guess you've been spending a lot of hours on your book. Or maybe at the dog pound."

"The Humane Society, you mean."

"Whatever." He stalked away.

Her eyes followed him as he entered the house, letting the screen door slam. He'd been sweet the night before and considerate during their love-making, even though he'd pressured her until she had given in. Something must have set him off, something besides the state of the barn. She could have spent more time going through Grandfather's junk, but she wasn't used to manual labor. Her body had ached at the end of each day no matter how much smelly stuff she rubbed into her muscles.

After ten or so minutes, Jeff returned, slurping at a cup he held in one hand, the other hand on his hip. The aroma of vanilla creamer and coffee filled the air. "I noticed you set some things aside. Anything for me?" He inclined his head at the pile she'd saved for him. His tone had become marginally kinder.

"I thought you might want to take a look at some stuff. If you don't think we need it, I can throw it away." She would have liked a cup of coffee.

"What's the pile just inside the doorway? An old desk? A dirty lamp? Some of those books and magazines look like they've been dragged through the dirt."

Aurora's stomach continued to spin. "I—I thought the credenza —it's not a desk—I thought once we had a real garage set up, there would be room inside to use the credenza to store stuff, like paper-work or tools."

His nose wrinkled, and he snorted. "We'll have a brand-new garage with a workbench and shelving. I'm not going to want to have an old piece of junk in there. Or the lamp either."

"I'm going to find a light bulb for the lamp and plug it in. If it works, I'll clean it up for my office."

"Really?" He gulped his coffee and laid the empty cup outside the doorway pile.

She shrugged. "I like the retro look."

"Aurora, you can't save everything you find in here. I guess you think you're going to read those old books and magazines?" He flapped his hand at her pile.

"At least look through them." She widened her eyes in what she hoped was a pleasant inquiring look. "Or not. There might be some interesting articles in the magazines."

"Maybe over the weekend you can spend a few minutes seeing if they're worth keeping and if not, dump them."

"Okay, Jeff, I will." She moved to the area she'd been working on the day before.

Jeff went to his pile and stood staring before going through everything, separating some things from the others. "Hey, I'm going to put the stuff I'm keeping on the vacant lot next door, just on the edge. The owners are never in town and won't know anyway, and the stuff I have outside already, around the side, too. I'll cover it with the tarp. Maybe tomorrow I won't have to fight off the nosy people who want to dig into everything."

"Sounds good." She didn't know why he was telling her all that after his attitude of a few minutes before. He obviously didn't care what she thought.

They worked all morning, broke for lunch, eating hoagie sandwiches she made and downing iced tea, and went at it again. The fall day was unseasonably warm, so Aurora had changed into a pair of cut-offs with her T-shirt and boots. Jeff had stripped down to just a pair of paint-splattered jeans and boots. Sweat streaked his dusted chest, and his body odor was apparent when she grew close.

A police car pulled into the driveway, and an officer got out. Aurora said, "That's the officer who came across the street and spoke to me the other day. The day they took the body out of the house."

Officer Dalton was in full uniform complete with his reflective sunglasses. His highly polished shoes kicked up the dust in the driveway as he approached.

Jeff pulled off his gloves and went out to meet the man, extending his hand. Aurora couldn't hear what was being said. She stopped what she'd been doing and walked out where they were.

"Hey, Mrs. Morris," the man said, removing his sunglasses.

Looking up at him, she held her hand above her eyes to shade them from the sun. She really needed to keep a hat in the barn. "Dalton, right? Quincy Dalton?"

"Yes, ma'am. I was about to tell your husband the little I'm allowed to say about the decedent across the street."

"I've been wondering," Aurora said, standing by Jeff's side and clasping his sweaty hand.

"Ordinarily we don't give out any information, but I explained to the chief about Mrs. Morris being by herself a lot." His eyes flicked from one to the other.

Jeff let go of Aurora's hand and slipped an arm around her shoulders.

"Who was it?" Aurora asked.

Dalton spread his legs and let his hand rest casually on the butt of his gun. "A woman who had rented the house a month or so ago. The landlord hadn't heard from her regarding the rent, so he called the constable for a welfare check."

"That's weird," Jeff said. "Why didn't he come himself?"

"Absentee landlord. He's from up around Amarillo. The house had been his mother's. He kept it for rental property."

Jeff cleared his throat. "His tenant was no relation to him?"

"None. He lists the house on the Internet. One of those short-term rental setups."

"Like VRBO," Aurora said. She leaned into Jeff. "I hope you're going to tell us she died from a heart attack, or she was sick, or something."

"I've said all I'm at liberty to say. I just wanted to let you know, so you could take precautions like we talked about the other day."

"Aurora filled me in on your conversation. I appreciate your concern," Jeff said. "I'm headed to the hardware store later this afternoon to get materials to shore up the windows and doors."

"Great. That'll go a long way to keeping your wife safe."

"I'm getting a dog." Aurora smiled up at Jeff. "On Monday."

"That's good to know." Dalton took a step back. "I'll be going."

"When will we be able to find out more?" Aurora asked.

"Don't know for sure. A detective's investigating. If he turns up something he thinks you need to know, I'm sure he'll inform you."

"And if not?" Aurora asked. "We just have to find out like everyone else?"

Jeff said, "I'm sure they're doing the best they can, Aurora. Give the guy a break."

Aurora wanted to remark *That's easy for you to say.* But she didn't. There was enough tension between them already for some unknown reason.

"Well, I'll take off." Dalton waved as he left, calling over his shoulder, "Take care."

Jeff dropped his arm from Aurora's shoulders. "I think I'll go to the hardware store now and get everything. I made a list earlier."

"Okay." She glanced back at the barn. Tired from spending the better part of the day working, Aurora wanted to quit and take a shower, but she was afraid Jeff would fuss at her. "I'll get back to work."

Jeff retrieved his sunglasses before going into the house for a few minutes. He came back out, having put on a T-shirt and clean pants. "Be back later." He threw her a kiss and climbed inside.

She must have been forgiven. She nodded and raised her hand toward him as he backed out of the driveway. As soon as he was gone, Aurora went inside for a break. She splashed water on her face and wiped away grit. After pouring herself a glass of iced tea, she sat for a few minutes, cooling down. She was beginning to have second thoughts about what they were doing. It was so much work. Hard work. But they'd agreed when they'd decided to buy out Harry and remodel.

When she finished her tea, she went back outside just as Sarah parked in the driveway. "I guess it's late enough for school to be out," Aurora said.

Sarah strode toward her. She still wore the denim jumper and blouse she called her teacher attire. "Well, yeah, it's almost five o'clock. Have you been out here all day? You look worn out."

"I am. Come into the barn out of the sun. There's a little pile of lumber we can sit on."

She glanced around. "Jeff's not here?"

"He went to the hardware store a little while ago."

"Good. We'll have time to talk. What did you want me to come over for last night?"

"You won't believe this, Sarah. Somebody died across the street. The police were here and everything." She sat on the pile of wood and indicated for Sarah to sit next to her.

"Great-God-almighty. What happened? Who lived there?"

"I don't know. I never saw more than an SUV parked there. Never saw anyone coming or going. The police asked me if I knew her, but I didn't have anything to tell them."

"Unbelievable. So, what did the cops say?" Sarah brushed at a one-by-ten and perched on it.

"Almost nothing. The officer who came and talked to me was here again today, not long ago, and still wouldn't give any details. But get this, he did say the lady didn't die of natural causes."

"That's not good!"

"No kidding. I feel really creeped out. Jeff's gone to buy better locks for the windows and doors."

"I'm glad he's at least doing that," Sarah said, sounding disgusted.

"What do you mean?" Sarah could be annoying, criticizing Jeff all the time, but still, Aurora valued her opinion.

"Well, Jeff's gone all the time."

Aurora slapped Sarah's knee. "He's working."

"Maybe he should get a job in town. If he was really concerned about you, he'd at least ask around about jobs."

"All right, Sarah, I know you don't like him."

"And he doesn't like me."

Aurora's eyes met Sarah's. "No comment. Anyway, I'll feel a lot better if he makes the house more secure. And, hey, he's letting me get a dog!"

"Letting you?" Sarah arched an eyebrow.

"You know what I mean. On Monday, when I go to volunteer, I'm going to pick one out. I'm going to talk to Taylor about it tomorrow when she comes to help with the sale."

"I know that'll make her happy. There are too dadgum many rescue dogs in this town. What kind do you want?"

"A big one." Aurora laughed. "Jeff's main requirement is the dog should be housebroken. I'm in agreement."

"Who wouldn't be? I'd hate to clean up after a big dog did his business inside."

They both giggled for a few moments. Aurora wiped the tears away.

"So, anyway," Sarah asked, "why'd you want me to come over last night?"

"I didn't know Jeff was coming home. I wanted to go across the street and peek in the windows to see what we could see."

"We can still do that after Jeff leaves again. I'd like to find out what went on, too. After all, you *are* my bestie. But you asked about my big flashlight? Don't you think the flashlights on our phones will be enough?"

"I don't know. I thought you had one of those high-powered ones. We could light up a whole room through a window."

"I do. Okay. Let's plan on it."

"Great. Why'd you stop by today? You plan to help set up for tomorrow?"

"Yeah, but I have something to tell you, too. I googled Ian Rawlings."

Aurora rubbed her palms together. "What'd you find?"

"Nothing. Well, that's not true. I found an Australian actor born in 1959. Too old. Besides there were lots of pictures. Definitely not him."

"That's weird. Are you sure you did it right?"

"How many ways can you google a person? You put their name in the search engine and wait for results."

"There was no one else with his name? It's kind of an unusual name, isn't it? With so many people in the world, though, I'm surprised there aren't more Ian Rawlings."

Sarah raised her right hand like she was about to take an oath. "I swear. There were some people named Rawlings but not him. They all had pictures, too. And some Rawlins—no G at the end of the name—but not him either."

"That's so strange. What about Linked In?"

"Same. I tried every place I could think of. I've heard of people being off the grid, and he's not, really, since he gave us his name and where he lives. He's just not on social media. But, come on, everyone is on something, Facebook, What's App, Instagram, TikTok . . . something.

"Unless that's not his real name. Didn't you say after you met him, you'd never seen him in town before?"

"Yeah. He said he was new to town, but if he bought a house and set up housekeeping and already bought some stuff to fix it up, seems like he would have been seen around town."

"Well, that's not necessarily true." Still, that information added to her uneasiness about Ian.

"I'm suspicious of anyone I can't find out about."

"I'm the mystery writer," Aurora said and laughed. "Makes me suspicious, too. Huh. He seems so nice."

"Yeah, huh. Are you thinking what I'm thinking?"

"I don't even want to go there."

"But what if he is? He could be. And I put my foot in it when I said what I said. Maybe that's why he stalked off."

"He just walked up to the barn. Besides, if he was a killer, he could have killed me when he came over here when I was alone." Aurora shivered.

"Maybe you're not his type. From what I've read, they do seem to kill certain types...well, I guess not all of them"

"You've been watching way too many true crime shows."

"Except we know there's one, at least one killer, in the Gulf Coast area, up and down I-45. No, wait, supposedly there's one closer to downtown Houston. They've found bodies in a bayou."

"I didn't know that. I probably should start watching local news more."

"Yeah, it's been all in the news. And one in the Austin area, but that won't affect us. They caught one of the Gulf Coast ones a while back. We've all read and heard about those cases. We need to get ahold of Georgina to find out if she's gotten the goods on the woman who was found on the side of the road near here last week."

Aurora hadn't read and heard about the cases Sarah was talking about, but then true crime wasn't her thing. "Gotten the goods?" She laughed. "You want to call Georgina to see if she's *gotten the goods*?"

"You know what I mean. I'm starting to feel really creeped out now, too. You know what I'm going to do?"

"Quit stalking him?"

Sarah stamped her foot. "That's not funny. Next time I see him, I'm going to take down his license plate number. Plus, I'm going to search online for owners of trucks like his make and model. And I'm going to look at the county deed records and see who his house is deeded to. And the tax records."

Aurora looked sideways at her friend. "Why are you so interested? He could just be a regular guy. Don't you have enough stuff to do teaching a room full of kids?"

"Probably, but just seeing he's not on social media has got me intrigued, if not a little nervous, scared."

"Sounds like a writerly thing to say. Are *you* writing a book now?" Aurora laughed again but could hear the nervousness in her own voice. Sarah needed to lighten up.

"Aurora, you need to take this more seriously. He's a stranger. He moves around. Anything is possible. You don't have to do anything. I'll let you know what I find."

"Just keep in mind if there have been recent real estate transactions, nothing may be on file yet."

"I'm going to do it anyway. Nowadays you can do it all online."

"I'm just glad I'm getting a dog. Here comes Jeff, back already. I need to get to work." Aurora stood.

"Yeah, before he cracks the whip on you," Sarah said with a smirk. "I'll see you tomorrow morning. I don't want to be around Jeff when no other people are around except you."

"Hey, will you contact Georgina and see if she'll be here tomorrow? We can find out what she knows then."

"Okay, I will."

As Sarah started for her car, Aurora called after her. "I'm just so amazed there was no record of him on the Internet anywhere."

"Me, too." Sarah took long strides. "Hey, Jeff." She waved to him. "See you tomorrow."

Carrying a plastic store bag in each hand, when Jeff reached Aurora, he asked, "What did *she* want?"

"She just stopped by to see if we could still use her help tomorrow." Aurora turned her back on him and strolled into the barn's interior, hoping he'd get the message. She wasn't interested in a discussion about her friend. No way she'd give up her relationship with her BFF just because Jeff didn't like her.

CHAPTER
TEN

"Do you have a plan for today?" Jeff asked the following morning as he poured himself a cup of coffee, the aroma of the fresh brew dominating the air. "Or a goal? We haven't really talked about when we want to get this barn project done. At least, not since we began." He wore his oldest, most worn out boots, the first pair of ripped jeans she had bought him, and a black muscle shirt.

Aurora wore a faded, red tank top, a pair of old ripped jeans as well, her boots, and her favorite, although shabby, light blue hoodie, which she'd remove once the temperature warmed up a bit. Though there'd been no rain, autumn was easing in almost unnoticed. Mornings were pleasant enough to make a person want to sit outside and breathe the cool air.

Her eyes raked over her husband's body, admiring his muscles. Even if there had been any time to do anything about any possible attraction, Aurora was still sore from his rough behavior of the night before. She didn't know what had gotten into him lately. When she'd tried to rebuff him, he'd become angry and kept after her, manhandling her until she gave in. He didn't seem to care how tired she was.

Leaning against the counter, she ate a bowl of sweetened oatmeal with raisins while they talked. She'd already had one cup of coffee and was contemplating pouring a second into a travel mug and taking it outside. "I was thinking if you want to plow through *your* side of the barn while I handle the sale, along with my friends who deign to show up, we could maybe only have one or two more sales." She spooned more cereal into her mouth and waited for his response. When he didn't say anything but just looked at her with a frown pulling at the sides of his mouth, she said, "You know I took the truck to the dump yesterday. Maybe we can fill it up with trash today. I'll take it to the dump again next week." She shoveled another spoonful of cereal into her mouth.

Rummaging in the large cardboard box temporarily serving as their pantry, Jeff came up with his favorite cold cereal, waving it in the air like he'd won a prize. "Found it." He dumped some cereal into a bowl. "Okay, I'm wondering. *Which* side of the barn is mine? Didn't know I had one." He raised an eyebrow and sneered, as he retrieved the milk from the refrigerator.

Swallowing twice, Aurora said, "The side you were clearing out yesterday, of course. I'm working on the far side, my side, and we can meet in the middle."

"We could put a FREE sign on what we consider trash. Maybe you wouldn't have to haul away so much stuff."

"Good idea. I'll print a sign." She put her bowl in the sink and glanced out the window. "Cars are pulling up. I'm going to brush my teeth and print the sign." She was also going to check on the puppy. She'd take the basket with her and leave it on the ground next to Georgina, who had agreed to be cashier again.

"I'll join you outside in a few minutes." Jeff perched on an old barstool.

In the few minutes it took Aurora to go outside, a number of cars had lined up on both sides of the street, and one blocked the drive-way. Word must have spread about the good deals, if people had a use for *retro* stuff. Calling it *retro* had been her brilliant idea. She'd written RETRO in capital letters on the new flyer.

Georgina and Taylor were just setting up the table near the entrance for Georgina to take the money. Sarah jogged up the driveway. Wearing clothes that looked like rejects from a thrift shop, her friends could have been street people. Aurora wasn't going to comment. Every day she worked in the barn, she looked like one, too.

"Hey, y'all," she called and waved as she carried the basket outside. "So glad to see you. Taylor, I wasn't sure you were coming."

Taylor yelled back, "And miss the free wine you're going to be handing out later? Wouldn't be anyplace else."

Aurora put the basket down next to the table. She hollered to the people who were lining up, "Five minutes. And whoever is blocking the driveway, please move your vehicle."

Sarah was breathless when she reached Aurora. "Sorry I'm late."

"You're not late. You're a volunteer. Volunteers are appreciated whenever they show up. Where do you want to be today?"

"I see Ian isn't here." Sarah scanned the crowd. "I didn't see his truck anywhere. Or at his house, either." She cocked her head like she thought his failure to appear was suspicious. "I'm guessing the white truck is Jeff's."

"We haven't even opened yet. Besides, Ian bought some trim and some other stuff the other day. He may not need anything else."

"Oh, I hope that's not true." They exchanged knowing looks. "So, what do you want me to do?"

"We've decided to make a pile to take to the dump and put this FREE sign on it. You want to help me inside the barn?" Sarah walked with her. "When we find something, could you carry it to the side of the yard between the tree and the driveway. When we get enough, it'll be easy to fill up the truck. I took a load the other day, but there's lots more."

"If that's what you want. I'm still hoping Ian will show up." Sarah glanced over her shoulder.

"I know you are. And if you know what's good for you, you'll think before you speak this week."

"Ha. Ha." Sarah shrugged one shoulder. "I will."

Aurora clapped her on the back. "Hey, I'm on your side. I hope we figure out who he is. If he's safe, you can go for it. Head on in."

"I will in a minute. I want to speak to Georgina." Sarah jogged back to the table at the entrance.

After trekking to where she'd positioned her canopy chair and plopping down, Taylor asked, "Is Monica coming?"

"She is, actually. She's supposed to stop by the store and buy some boxed wine for our enjoyment later."

Taylor looked sideways at Aurora.

"Hey, just because all we've been having on Mondays is bottled wine doesn't mean boxed wine isn't any good. There are some tasty, boxed wines."

"That was my teasing look," Taylor said. "I've had boxed wine. I hope she gets the right ones, though."

"Next time you can get the wine if you want a specific brand. By the way, don't let any of our customers hear us. We're not throwing a party for the whole town. So, are you comfortable?"

"For now." Taylor patted the arm of her chair. "Thank you. Today is supposed to be sunny and clear. I burn so easily."

Aurora touched Taylor's already warm cheek. "I know. I just think it's funny you brought your own chair this week. We have chairs."

"Bet you don't have one like this. With a roof on it." She burst out with loud laughter. "Don't mind me. I had a good morning before I arrived."

"I'm not even going to ask who and to what you're alluding." Aurora looked back at the house.

"I'm bad," Taylor said. "Anyway, what exactly do you want me to do from this spot?"

"I know our stuff is mostly, or—at least a lot of—junk but watch to make sure no one is pocketing anything. Also, if they need a container, could you grab them a box from behind the barn? We piled some up yesterday. And tell them we have bags down where Georgina is. Or, if they need one—if they have their hands full of stuff—could you run get one for them?"

"Whoa, that's a tall order." Taylor laughed again. "Not really."

Aurora had to smile. Taylor really was in a good mood. "I know you can handle it. I just had an idea. I'm going to run down and talk to Georgina, too, before she moves my crime scene tape. Thanks."

Holding the puppy, Sarah sat down next to Georgina in one of the collapsable chairs. Georgina had brought her own folding chair, which she claimed was better for her back. "So how are you this morning, Georgina? Ready to begin?"

"Hey, ma'am, when are you opening up?" A man hollered.

Aurora could swear he was the same man from the week before. "In a minute," she yelled back. "Keep your pants on."

"Remember Georgina forgot to give you the money from last week?" Sarah cut her eyes over at Georgina. "You gotta love her, but sometimes...anyway, she brought it all back with her this week. I was going to take the box inside and put the larger bills away someplace. Or, you want to do that?"

"I heard what you said, and I'm sorry," Georgina spoke in a voice only Sarah and Aurora could hear. "I've had a lot on my mind." She murmured, "Remind me, when no one's around, to tell you what I learned about the murdered woman."

"The woman across the street? She was murdered?" Aurora asked, wondering whether she was getting an ulcer since her stomach felt raw again.

"I don't know about her yet. The autopsy isn't back. I meant the one they found by the road last week."

"Yuck," Sarah and Aurora said at the same time.

"Go ahead and take the box, Sarah," Aurora said. "I'll stay here with Georgina. If we need change before you're back, I'll come and get you. It shouldn't take you more than a few minutes to hide the money away."

"Don't tell her anything until I return," Sarah said.

"Okay." Georgina pulled her hair up into a clip and straightened in her chair.

"Is Jeff in the house?" Sarah asked. "I guess I'll yell before I enter." She took the box and handed the puppy to Aurora.

Snuggling the puppy in her left arm, Aurora jerked the crime scene tape with her right, so it fell off the tree behind them. "Okay, folks. Sorry to keep you waiting. Come on in." Once everyone had crossed over, she'd pull the tape from the other side and roll it up for the next sale.

"I still think it's funny you use crime scene tape," Georgina said.

"Did I tell you last week a couple of people asked about it? I told them I write mysteries and gave them a card with my website on it. If I already had a book out, I probably could have sold some copies." She sat down in the chair next to Georgina. "Tell me what's got you so rattled."

They waited a few minutes while the first wave of customers and some stragglers entered, then Georgina said, "I'm not really rattled. I'm not that bad. But I've been thinking about the dead woman a lot."

"The one by the road. Did y'all learn something new?"

"We should wait for Sarah."

"I'll fill her in later," Aurora said, leaning in close to Georgina.

Georgina hesitated a moment and watched the people before answering. "We're always learning something new, but I don't always hear about it until later if it's not my case. Sometimes I hear snatches here and there."

"What's got you concerned about the snatches you heard?"

"Several things. You know how those guys mow the tall weeds beside the roadways?"

"That's how they found the dead woman?"

"No, not the one we were talking about last week. They found a body farther in, away from the road. The man riding the mower spotted her. They thought she might have been there for a week or so."

Aurora cringed and studied Georgina's stricken face. Could the person who had been in her barn the week before somehow be connected with the two women found near the road and the woman across the street?

"They're wondering whether she was killed by the same person." She hooked her arm in Aurora's and whispered. "There could really be a serial killer roaming around our neck of the woods, like the man who grabbed those girls, like whoever put bodies in the killing fields in League City a long time ago."

"I thought they caught him. But maybe not. They could be coincidences," Aurora said, uneasy. Seemed like there had to be a connection.

"The department wants to tell women to be extra careful, but they're afraid to alarm people more than necessary."

"I can see why that's keeping you on edge."

Monica arrived carrying two boxes of wine, one in each hand. "Want me to put these inside?"

"Sure, if you don't mind," Aurora said. "Want me to come with you?"

"Nah. Jeff in there?"

"He was. I don't know if he still is. Sarah went to stash the cash. She might still be there, but it shouldn't be taking her this long."

"Stash the cash?" Monica did an eye roll and walked on to the back door.

Georgina waited until Monica was out of hearing range and continued. "The biggest thing is the description of the woman. She was a millennial like us. Like the other woman. I told the guys in the department I thought they had an obligation to let the public know what's going on."

"Yeah, me too. I mean, isn't there a range of ages with missing women? At least, that's what I've always heard."

"You're right. One guy said he thought most of the victims were millennials, at least the recent ones. Like someone had something against women our age. Maybe the guy—they're assuming it's a guy. It's always a guy who kills women and girls, right? The man could have a vendetta against our age group. FBI says the same thing. I'm trying to get my hands on the full FBI report."

"The FBI is involved? Have they been at the department? Have you talked to them or heard what they've said?"

Georgina's eyes shifted to a couple of new people walking up. "There's a report."

"Their report would definitely make for interesting reading." Aurora stroked the puppy's little body, her mind racing. Georgina's information was good for two reasons. First, for their group's safety, and of course other people's, too, and second, for whether or not she would want to include a serial killer in her book. Call it research. Creepy research.

"But wait 'til I tell you the worst thing," Georgina said, her hand in front her mouth. She glanced at a few more late-comers.

"Good morning. Go right up. There will be people at the barn to help, if you need any," Aurora said, gesturing toward Taylor.

"Anyway," Georgina said, cupping her hand over her mouth again and turning away from the path, her head down. "I found out why they suspect at least some of the women were killed by the same person."

Aurora swiveled away from the drive and toward Georgina, ducking her head, as well, so people wouldn't overhear them. "How did you find out if it's not your case?"

"Um, well, I'm seeing someone." A small smile appeared on her face.

"Oh, one of the cops? I thought your denial the other day was rather weak. So, he tells you what's going on?"

"Sometimes by accident, but yes. You know him, by the way."

"Me? I don't know any police officers."

"He was here yesterday. Quincy Dalton."

"You're kidding me." Aurora shook her head. "No wonder he

seemed a little less formal than I thought an investigating officer would be. Does he know we're friends?"

Nodding, Georgina said, "Yes. And he's not the investigating officer or anything. I call him a beat cop, but you know in a small town like ours, sometimes we wear more than one hat."

"He's kind of cute," Aurora said, "if you like cops, and it looks like you do. Anyway, what has he told you about the woman they found the other day?"

"You can't tell anyone he told me this stuff. Someone might know it came from him."

"No problem." Aurora poked Georgina's arm. "You have to tell me first."

"What the killer is doing, they think, is strangling these women."

"That's not unusual, is it?"

"He strangles them and then throws them out on the street and runs over them."

Aurora flinched. "Throws them? That's awful. How creepy. Is that what happened to both the women you're talking about?"

"Let's them go, throws them, whatever. I don't know about the most recent one. She was only just discovered. But the one they found outside of Houston a few months back, yeah."

"Dalton probably told you about my neighbor across the street, right?"

Georgina cocked her head and nodded. A departing couple walked past them. "Bye," Georgina said, and Aurora did the same.

"That can't be what happened to her, my neighbor. Her body was found in the house."

"She wasn't strangled." Georgina rubbed a finger over her lips. "At least there were no obvious signs."

"How'd she die then?" Aurora asked. "Your boyfriend wouldn't tell us."

Georgina's smile brightened her face. "He's not my boyfriend. Yet. We've only gone out a few times."

"You're not going to tell me? I really want to know. I *need* to know."

"I wish I could tell you, but I haven't found out. I knew about a body being in the house, because Quince told me, but he wouldn't say much else. I only heard her death wasn't like the others."

Someone trudged over the driveway rocks and cleared his throat. "Hello, ladies. Is this where you pay?"

Aurora and Georgina both straightened up. The man held a pile of short two-by-fours that most people would consider trash.

"Yes, sir," Georgina said.

"I'll talk to you later," Aurora said. "Sarah can stay with you to keep you company, if you need any." Aurora put the puppy back in the basket. Thinking how glad she was she was getting a dog on Monday, she headed to the barn, letting the man and Georgina discuss prices. Georgina was really good at negotiations.

"I've been with Jeff," Sarah said, coming from the direction of the barn. "Well, not really *with* him, but I was standing near him while he's been negotiating with a man who wants to buy all the doors." Grinning, she held the money box under her arm.

Aurora shook her head. Sarah was probably looking over Jeff's shoulder just to annoy him. "Boy, selling all the doors would be great. You want to keep Georgina company for a little while? She's kind of jumpy. She can tell you why."

Sarah headed for Georgina, past the trash pile. Aurora heard her laugh and say to a man, "If you want some of it, you have to take all of it. At least what's there right now. We won't make you take what we'll be putting there later."

Aurora flapped her hand at Taylor and went into the barn. People poked around, digging through layers. The woman who'd bought a stack of windows the week before, stood in front of another stack on Aurora's side of the barn. "Didn't you take some of these last week?" Aurora asked, approaching her.

The woman had her hair pinned back, her sleeves rolled up, and her jeans cinched at the waist with a brown leather belt. She thumbed through the windows like one would a row of LP records in an antique store. "I'm checking to see if this bunch in the front have any broken glass."

"I think you said last week you decorate them with flowers and mirrors and sell them at trade fairs?"

"You wouldn't think many people would want stuff like this, but they do. They like a *country* look." She glanced at Aurora and chuckled. Her eyes were hazel with green specks. "How much if I take every last one of the windows?"

"Oh, my, I don't know. Do you need so many?"

"I have a storage shed. I'm thinking I would work on them all winter and have some done for every trade show I go to in the spring. Are you interested?"

"Shoot, yeah. You must have seen there're a lot back there. If you want all of them, can I interest you in taking those once we dig them out?"

"If we can make a deal." She gave Aurora the side eye, but not in a mean-spirited way, more like a little bird looking at something with curiosity. Maybe even a little devilishly. She rubbed her lips together, eyes shining.

Aurora chewed on the inside of her cheek. She could talk to Jeff about it, but Jeff was standing in front of a stack of doors and apparently still negotiating over them. "You would give me some time to dig them out? I mean, you wouldn't expect me to let you have them immediately? It's not like I can spend every day pulling out stuff to get to the windows."

"No problem. I'll take some today, and when you get a bunch, you can call me to come fetch them. Okay?"

"Sounds good. Why don't you wait outside under the tree where there's a little breeze, and we can talk about money? I want to speak to my husband."

"Sure thing."

Tugging on Jeff's arm, Aurora smiled at the man Jeff had been talking to and held up one finger. "I'll just be a minute."

Turning toward Aurora, Jeff said, "What is it?" A muscle in his jaw flexed. "Something wrong? I'm trying to sell the doors to this gentleman."

"I'm making a deal on all the windows. You don't have a problem with that, do you?"

He glanced over her shoulder toward the stack of windows. When he looked back at her, his grim expression broke into a thin smile. "You think you're up to negotiating a big sale?"

Surprised he would doubt her, she nodded. "Just when I was getting tired of holding these sales. The lady is outside. She's giving me some time to pull out the ones in the back. She'll take all of them."

Jeff peered over Aurora's shoulder toward her side of the barn a second time.

"Everything all right with you?" Aurora asked.

"Fine." He buffed her cheek. "You know you'll have to sort them out by yourself. I won't be around to help. Make sure she'll wait long enough you won't have to kill yourself doing it."

"I will, Jeff." Or not, she thought as she jogged outside to negotiate with the woman. Before long, Jeff and she would be through with the barn, get it torn down, and start building the house they'd live in for the rest of their lives. At least that was her plan, and she was determined to carry it out. Maybe then he'd go back to treating her like he did when they first met, dazzling her with his charm.

CHAPTER

ELEVEN

As soon as Jeff left Monday morning, Aurora poured herself a cup of coffee and fired up her computer to google Ian. Surely Sarah hadn't been completely thorough. Aurora hadn't searched over the weekend for fear Jeff would, for some unknown reason, look on her computer and see what she'd been doing and use what he found to chastise her. Anyway, she had a hard time believing Ian Rawlings had no social presence.

Finding nothing through Google, she went to Facebook. Again, nothing. Linked In, nothing. Instagram, nothing. TikTok, nothing. YouTube, What's App and on and on whatever she could think of. Half an hour later, she gave up. When she had more time, she'd ask the Internet to give her any other places she could search.

Just for fun, she googled Jeff. There were several Jeff Morris's but none him. Opening Facebook again, she searched Facebook and found nothing. Strange. Was it just a thing? Did some men around her age not do social media as much as women?

Seeing the time was getting away from her, Aurora decided to focus on her novel, get something done before leaving for The Humane Society. She wasn't going to give up, though. She and Sarah would continue to put their heads together to try to figure Ian out. And she'd ask Jeff when he called why he wasn't on social media. He had a cell phone. She'd seen him lose himself once he sat down with his own laptop.

Since Ian hadn't come to the second sale on Saturday, they'd been unable to get his license plate number. Sarah told Aurora she'd *accidentally* driven by his house both Saturday and Sunday, but his truck wasn't there. Sarah was determined to find out more about Ian, who she now called *The Stranger*.

After a bag of salad for lunch, Aurora grabbed the basket of puppy and drove to The Humane Society. When Taylor opened the door to meet her, the doggie odor was so strong, Aurora felt like she'd been hit with a blast of heat. The place really needed a thorough cleaning and airing out.

Taylor was all grins. "Give me the puppy." She snatched the basket out of Aurora's hand and peered inside. "I think she's thrived under your care. Come with me to my office."

"First, you know I've taken good care of her. Second, what's going on?"

Monica sat in front of Taylor's desk, with a child in the chair next to her.

"What are you doing here?" Aurora eyed the child.

"Let me introduce my daughter, Ava. Remember I mentioned her last week?"

Ava said, "Hello." She had curly black hair and almost ivory skin. Her blue eyes sparkled as she focused on the basket hanging from Taylor's hand. Her little jeans were rolled up in cuffs. She wore a matching pink T-shirt the same color as the tennis shoes on her feet. "Is this the puppy?" A hopeful expression covered her face as she looked from Taylor to Aurora.

"What's going on?" Aurora asked.

Monica said, "Last Saturday when you told everyone about getting a dog, I thought maybe Taylor would let us have this puppy for Ava. Taylor said you're only fostering the pup?"

Aurora's eyes inexplicably teared up. She looked away and blinked rapidly. Jeff didn't want her to keep the puppy, but in the week she'd had the tiny thing, she'd grown attached. Still, if she was going to get a big dog, maybe she shouldn't have a little baby, one a big dog might not like. She glanced from Monica to Taylor to Ava. Aurora crouched down and took the child's little soft hand in her own. "Nice to meet you, Ava. How old are you?"

"Eight." She stood on her tiptoes and peeked into the basket. "Awww, isn't she cute?"

"She requires a lot of attention right now and sleeps a lot. You'll have to keep her clean and warm and fed." Aurora stood up. "Can you do this big job? And who will care for her while you're in school?"

"My dad's a firefighter. He's home a lot and would look after her on the days he's home, and I'm at school. Can I hold her, Miss Taylor?"

"Sit back in the chair," Taylor said and placed the basket in Ava's lap.

Ava picked up the pup and held her to her cheek. The pup's fur and Ava's hair matched like they were color coded. Maybe that was a sign. Aurora smiled at the thought. She didn't believe in signs. "What about the days your father is at the fire department?"

"He works one on and two off," Monica said, "so it wouldn't be much of a problem. He can take her to the station. The guys would love her to death."

Aurora crossed her arms. "That's what I'm afraid of. Taylor, don't you think she shouldn't be handled much?"

Taylor took Aurora's arm. "It'll be okay. They'll take good care of her. Don't look so sad." She grinned. "So, it's settled. Monica, go up front. There're some papers you need to fill out. Ava, put the pup back in the basket."

"Don't even ask me if she can keep my basket," Aurora said to Taylor. "Of course you can, Ava. I know you'll be a good caretaker of this little baby." Aurora stroked the puppy's head. "Maybe sometime you'll let me come visit her?" She said a silent goodbye to the puppy. She was glad she hadn't named her.

"Yes, ma'am," Ava said. "Can I go now?"

"Yes," Taylor said. "Join your mom. I have other business with Miss Aurora." She took Aurora's arm again, leading her into the back area of the building where the doggie smell was even stronger, and the dogs were barking their heads off.

Aurora's eyes watered again, but this time from the odor. As soon as she entered the caged-in back area, some of the dogs began jumping up and down and barking. Her heart went out to all of them. Too many throwaway dogs.

"Oh, Taylor, there are more than last week. Poor little things."

"There are. Another raid at another house." She sighed audibly. "Somebody kept way more animals than they could take care of. From the description of the premises, it was enough to make you sick to your stomach. Anyway, the raid was a few days ago. We've managed to place some of the animals in other towns and bathe and get medical care for the ones we've kept here. See any you'd want to take home with you?"

"Try all of them." Aurora paced to the end of the cages and back. "I was thinking a female. And, of course, she has to be spayed and house broken."

"I have a couple of candidates I thought you might like." As they passed the first cage, Taylor said, "This one's a male." She stopped in front of the second cage.

A black, fluffy, mid-sized dog with a long snout and pleading brown eyes stood on her hind legs and stuck her nose through the chain link fencing.

Aurora scratched the dog's nose. "She looks really sweet." The dog licked her fingers.

"She is. Let's go to the next one."

The second female had to be a cross between a dachshund and something else. She was short-haired and low to the ground and had floppy ears and a short snout, almost like a pug's. When she barked, however, Aurora stepped back. Certainly, anyone entering a house where that dog resided would hesitate. The dog continued barking and then squatted and peed.

Jeff, for sure, wouldn't be happy with a dog whose barking couldn't be controlled and certainly not with one who might not be fully house broken. "Hmmm, I'm thinking she might not be a good fit for us."

Taylor said, "She's sweet when she you get to know her."

"I don't think so." She glanced at the next pen. A coffee-colored, mid-sized dog, with a plastic cone around her head, sat in the corner. When Aurora approached, the dog limped to the fence just out of reach of Aurora's fingers. The dog held one of her hind legs up off the floor, a bandage on its foot. "What happened to her?"

"We're not sure. I was told all the animals weren't penned. Some ran wild in the street. We think she might have gotten too close to a car, and her paw was run over. A couple of her toes were smashed and had to be amputated."

"Awww." Aurora whistled softly and called to the animal. "Come here, girl."

The dog took a step closer and shivered.

Aurora asked, "Will she bite if I put my fingers through the wire?"

"Not so far." Taylor laughed.

Aurora said, "Not funny." She crouched down, so her eyes were level with the dog's light brown, almost amber, eyes, and turned aside, not looking directly into the dog's eyes, but up at Taylor.

"She's watching you," Taylor said. She reached her hand into one of her pockets and pulled out a treat, giving it to Aurora.

The dog put her nose up to the wire.

"Better toss it, Aurora. Give her a chance to trust you."

Aurora called out, "I'm your friend," and dropped the treat over the top of the fence. She watched as the dog plucked the treat off the floor and stepped back to the fencing.

"Would you want a dog, an injured dog, who is missing toes? What would Jeff say?" Taylor asked.

"He said to get whatever kind I wanted. He knew I was coming here to get a rescue. Do you think I should take her?"

"It would be nice if you would. A lot of people wouldn't, since she's missing parts of her foot. But if you do, know it's going to be a few more days before you can take the bandage off. You might have to re-bandage it."

"She does look sweet, not aggressive, not a barker like the girl over there—who's watching like she's hoping I'll adopt her."

"They all are. If you decide on this one, here's what I can do. We'll bathe her again this afternoon and re-bandage her paw, and I'll bring her to you tonight. We're still meeting at your place?"

"Hmmm, hard decision." She smiled at the dog and could swear the dog smiled back. "She is spayed? And housebroken?"

"Yes. And she's been totally good while she's been here. Never had an accident. She waits until one of the volunteers takes her outside, or if she really wants to go, she'll bark a couple of times. You know how it is. You've been here. Anyway, we think she might have been loved by someone before she ended up at that horrible house."

Aurora took a deep breath of doggy odor and exhaled. Adopting a dog was a big decision, but she really liked the look of the girl before her. "Could you open the cage, and we'll see if she likes me as much as I like her?"

Taylor did and stepped inside, in front of Aurora. "This is Aurora," Taylor said, bending down and scratching the dog's head. The dog licked Taylor's face, eliciting a chuckle. Looking up at Aurora, Taylor said, "She might be kind of shy, at first. Another reason for me to bring her to you. She already knows me."

"Can I come in now?" Aurora had her hand on the gate for security, but she didn't sense she would need to back away,

"Sure. Slowly, though."

Aurora took a couple of baby steps inside and crouched down. The dog faced her and stared for a few moments before she stepped close. She looked from one woman to the other.

Taylor stood. "Well, she's not afraid of you."

"Why would she be? She's almost bigger than I am. May I have another snack?"

Taylor slipped another treat into Aurora's hand. Aurora wasn't sure if she should look the dog in the eye yet, so she held out her palm and allowed the dog to take the treat. "You're going to have to give me the name of these, so I can get the same kind."

"Will do."

"And I need someone to put in a dog run on the side of the house, because we have no real fence."

"I have just the guy."

"Can you point me to the right pet store to go to for supplies?"

"Of course, I will." Taylor laughed. "So, yes?"

"I'm going to call her Chloe."

"Just one thing to remember. If the way her toes got hurt was from chasing cars, you need to be real careful. She can't be outside without being on a leash unless she's in the dog run—once you get a dog run."

"Don't worry," Aurora said. "I'll take real good care of her."

AFTER HER SHIFT at the shelter, Aurora drove across town to the pet store. She couldn't keep the smile off her face as she looked at the list of things she wanted to buy for Chloe. A cushy bed, for one thing. And a leash, so she could walk her, though she had an idea Chloe might be walking her. Taylor had given Aurora some tips. It's one thing to walk a little dog and let them have their head, but a larger dog needed to be trained to walk beside the owner. Dogs need to know who's boss, Taylor said.

Inside the pet store, when she reached for a basket, Aurora came face-to-face with Ian who held a humongous bag of dog food in his arms.

"Hey, Aurora. What are you doing on this side of town? Don't tell me you're getting a pet."

"We missed you last Saturday," Aurora said. "I hope you didn't want any windows and doors, we've sold them all." She grinned. "I'm getting a dog. My friend Taylor is bringing her over this evening." A little voice told her if he was the serial killer he'd avoid her house once she had a dog, though the killer in the recent news didn't go to people's houses—he just picked them up somewhere. Where, she didn't yet know.

He hefted the dog food bag up onto his shoulder, revealing a developed bicep. "What kind are you getting?"

"A brown one." Good thing he couldn't read her mind.

He chuckled. "I meant what breed?"

"I would call her a mosaic dog."

"Okay, I get it. So, you're here to buy all your supplies?" He pointed to the bag on his shoulder. "Think about this brand. Gerhard scarfs it down as fast as he can."

"Well, that's a high recommendation coming from Gerhard. I'll check it out. I'd better take a basket and get busy. My friends are coming over tonight, so I need to be home soon."

"Good seeing you. Good luck with…"

"Chloe. Her name is Chloe."

"By the way, where's Jeff off to this week? Or is he in town? There's something I wanted to speak to him about."

She shrugged. She really ought to pay more attention when Jeff said where he was heading. "I think someplace like South Texas, but I really don't know. Is there something I could ask him when he calls tonight?"

"Nah. Nothing important."

"Okay. Hey, I was just thinking, maybe when Chloe's settled, you could bring Gerhard over for a playdate."

Ian laughed. "Like a couple of kids. That's certainly something to consider. He shoved the door open and exited to the parking lot.

Aurora almost slapped herself in the head. What was she doing asking a man to come over to her house when Sarah suspected him of being a killer? Was she out of her mind? He didn't even mention where he'd been on Saturday, why he wasn't at their sale, or whether he was disappointed they'd sold all the doors and windows. He wasn't answerable to her, but now her curiosity was aroused even more. Where did he go on the weekend? If Sarah had driven by his house on Saturday evening after he didn't show up at the sale, or Sunday, and seen any sign of him, she would have told Aurora. So, what could be up with Ian?

CHAPTER

TWELVE

After arriving home, Aurora set up the bowls and bed for Chloe and put everything else away. She changed into her grungy clothes and boots. Donning some work gloves, she went to the barn to make a dent in the remaining windows. Though it hadn't rained earlier, in spite of the sky clouding up, the temperature was still mild enough to make working in the barn not too tedious.

She'd be glad to get rid of the windows, to work deeper in the barn where the wind wouldn't blow so much dust and dirt onto her body and into her hair and eyes. Of course, no breeze meant the smell of old, decaying stuff hung in the air constantly. She'd moved some windows into the yard under the tree on Sunday and cleared a path to the rest, but by then, she'd grown tired. Jeff had called to her, so Aurora stopped and went into the house. Jeff had already showered and changed and pulled some food out of the refrigerator for her to cook for Sunday dinner.

Later in the evening, she'd been unable to convince Jeff she was too tired to have sex. When he didn't want to take no for an answer, she thought of it as sex, not making love. Her first husband had been demanding, though he'd become less so over time, which she found out later was because he'd been with her best friend. She supposed she should be grateful Jeff continued to be insistent. She had been grateful, at first, but once the honeymoon was over—figuratively speaking—and she'd lost the baby, and they'd moved, something changed, or she felt it did. Rough sex was not her thing. When she'd mentioned she'd like him to be a little gentler, he had been, at first.

Sometimes, Aurora wanted to smack herself in the head. She not only questioned her choice in men, but she questioned *why* she made such choices. She'd never admit to anyone, even Sarah, that maybe she'd jumped into this marriage too fast. But then, she had been pregnant. Her nature wasn't to have a baby *out-of-wedlock,* as her grandmother would have put it.

Now, with a couple of hours to spare before the Monday evening meeting, she approached her task, pleased with herself when she stopped to admire how empty the building was becoming, relatively speaking. Jeff had made short shrift of the doors on Saturday, helping the man fill up his truck and practically kissing him goodbye.

She'd push herself to get all the windows ready to be picked up and be done with it. Tuning her phone to a podcast, she set it down before tackling the first one. Brushing the dirt and loose paint off a single paned window, she put it under the tree where they'd positioned so many items for the first sale. Behind the single-paned, was a double-hung, the glass loose in the frame. Being super careful not to do anything to jeopardize the glass, Aurora dragged it slowly out of the barn to the tree and set it up on the other side from the single-paned ones. Out of breath, she stopped and shook out her gloves.

Across the street, the crime scene tape waved back and forth in the breeze. There had been no more action at her former neighbor's house. She and Sarah were planning on sneaking there on Tuesday night to see what they could see. They didn't want their idea pooh-poohed, so they wouldn't tell their other friends, especially Georgina.

In her heart, Aurora wished the cops would remove the tape, and the landlord would have the house cleaned and rented again. The empty building was creepy, the way it sat there, an empty vessel which, in the night under illumination from the moon, looked a great deal like a skeleton head, only way bigger.

Shivering, she turned her back on the incident site and pulled her gloves back on. Tuning to some jazz, she perked up and quickened her step. She couldn't wait to have Chloe. Aurora would feel less creeped out when there was a warm body, even a dog's warm body, keeping her company.

She took hold of the second two-paned window, this one being another double-hung, checking to be sure the sash lock was connected, so the window would hold together when she dragged it. Something prevented the lower part of the window from closing, and when she looked closer, Aurora found a knife, a huge pocketknife. The knife's long blade was jammed in the window. She tried to dislodge it but succeeded only in drawing back gloved fingers with a brown substance on them. "Yuck," she said aloud. Dirt? Rust? Some other kind of corrosion? She wiped her gloves on the leg of her pants before going inside to get a damp rag to wrap around the handle to get a better grip.

What an odd thing to discover. Weirder than the rabbit head. And the larger skeleton head. Weirder than the snakeskin. A knife. What would be next? In her wild imagination, what she liked to think of as her mystery writer brain, she wondered if the next thing would be a body? She laughed at herself. Thankfully, there was no room in all her grandfather's junk for a human body.

Returning with a dishrag, she grabbed the knife by the handle with both hands. No amount of tugging succeeded. Frustrated, Aurora gave up and dragged the window to one side so she could access the others. She worked another half an hour and was about to call it quits when a youngish man drove up in a truck, all the way across the open area to where the grass began and started unloading chain-link fencing materials.

"Hey," she hollered as she strode toward him. "What do you think you're you doing?"

The man wore jeans, a blue work-shirt with the sleeves rolled up, a gimme cap embossed with a lumber company emblem, and dirty running shoes. He stopped, his hands resting on a roll of fencing. "Unloading stuff, so I can build your fence."

"I didn't order fencing. What's your name?"

"Sebastion, but you can call me Bastion."

Ready to challenge him, Aurora stood with her hands on her hips. "Well, Bastion, I didn't order anything from your company, if what's on your cap is the name of your company."

"No, ma'am, Miss Taylor placed the order."

"Miss Taylor from the animal shelter?" Had Taylor and she discussed ordering materials for a fence? Jeff had been accusing her of being forgetful lately, but she only remembered saying she didn't have a fence and would have to keep Chloe inside until Jeff okayed having one installed.

He nodded. "Said for us to build a dog run at the side of your house from the bayou to the street with a gate facing the back door." He indicated the far side of Aurora's house, where there wasn't much other than a strip of land with weeds Jeff mowed about every other weekend.

"That's news to me. When did she call y'all?"

"This morning." He lifted the fencing, ready to continue with his task. "Can I go ahead? It's fixing to get dark."

Aurora laughed. She had told Taylor she was going to pick out a dog and, apparently, Taylor had taken her at her word even before Aurora showed up to choose one. "All right. I guess so."

What would Jeff say when she told him in their nightly phone call. She'd planned to just talk about the dog. Jeff would demand to know who was going to pay for the fence. To alleviate an argument, Aurora would volunteer her own money, what was left from her inheritance. Jeff had to know a dog would require a fenced-in area. At least, that's what she'd tell him.

The man carried metal fence material to the side yard while Aurora stood for a few minutes and watched. As she turned to go back to the porch, her friends began to arrive. Car after car after truck began pulling up and parking parallel to her property. Only one drove into the yard. Taylor's van.

Aurora jogged to Taylor once she parked. She slid open the van's side door, and Chloe hopped down into the yard. Taylor clipped a leash to Chloe's collar and handed it to Aurora.

Chloe had been bathed and her chocolate brown coat fluffed. After a moment of surprise and a glance at the wide grin on Taylor's face, Aurora crouched down and spoke to Chloe and patted her. She smelled of lavender. "What did you do, spray her with dog perfume?" Aurora asked when she stood.

"After bathing her with scented dog shampoo." Taylor preened, pleased with herself.

"You're impossible, and I'm not just talking about foo-fooing the dog." Aurora looked over her shoulder. "What's with the fence?"

Taylor reached into the van and retrieved her shoulder bag and a bottle of wine. "We have grant money to pay for fencing when people who adopt animals don't have a fence."

Aurora didn't believe her for a minute. "Uh-huh. How come no one ever mentioned that before now?" She walked beside Taylor. Chloe walked beside Aurora, not frisky, more like apprehensive. Aurora reached down and scratched the top of Chloe's head and was rewarded with what could have been a grin.

"You've only been volunteering for a short while. You can't know everything we do at the shelter." Taylor waved at the other women who had arrived. "Hey, Monica, Sarah, how are y'all doing?"

Aurora crouched down again to Chloe, and said, "Do we believe her, Chloe? Should we just leave the subject alone? Should we be grateful for her help?"

"I can hear you," Taylor called. "And yes, just leave it alone. We, at the shelter, are happy you adopted Chloe."

"Ahh," Monica said when Aurora and Chloe climbed the steps to the porch. "She looks like a chocolate tumbleweed, kind of latte."

"A tumbleweed is a good description? More like a woolly sheep, I think," Aurora said.

Sarah said, "She's a cute dog, but can she bark? You need a barker in case someone comes onto your property."

"In time," Taylor said. "Give her time to get settled in. There's a 3-3-3 rule." Taylor launched into an explanation. "Initially, three days—"

"Never mind," Sarah said. "I don't need the course. Save it for Aurora." Holding a bottle of wine, she went inside the house.

"We already covered it," Taylor called after her.

"Georgina isn't coming tonight. I saw her at lunch, and she told me to tell y'all," Monica said.

Sarah came outside and said, "I wish Georgina would be here. I wanted to hear the latest on the serial killer."

"We don't know it's a serial killer," Taylor said. She took a wine glass from the ones Sarah held in her hands and reached for an opened bottle of wine.

"Yeah, we do," Sarah said. "Want me to reiterate what we've learned?"

Monica said, "Too gross. Do we always have to talk about murdered women?"

"Not always, but Mondays are a good time to catch up with what's been going on, except Georgina isn't here to catch us up."

"And there hasn't been anything in our little paper," Aurora said. She took a swallow of the white wine Sarah had brought, washing away some grit.

"Or in the Houston Chronicle," Sarah said. "I've been searching online and in the printed version to see what I can find. Nada."

Monica said, "I've heard something." All the other women turned their attention on her. "They think he *is* a serial killer and lives in the Houston area. He's moved his territory, though, they think to throw off any investigators. At least, that's what's going around at the fire department."

"And you know that how?" Sarah asked.

"Because when they find bodies, the EMTs go out and the fire-fighters go with them, so Tommy and the guys have been talking about it. He says he'd like to lock us in the house until the guy is caught," Monica said.

"Like that's going to happen," Aurora said, "but Monica's right. A fire truck came across the street when my neighbor woman was found dead."

"Like what's going to happen? His getting caught, or us being locked in a house?" Taylor asked.

"Yeah, no, whatever," Monica said. "But I promised to be careful and to warn all my friends to be careful. So, be careful."

"Y'all are giving me the willies," Sarah said.

Taylor said, "What if the killer has moved more than his territory? What if he's moved to the suburbs, like here?"

"Ha. Ha. Very funny," Sarah said. "What's worse than the willies? Because I'm feeling whatever that is."

THIRTEEN

Aurora had turned down her phone when her friends were over and missed Jeff's call. In a terse text, he said he'd call the following day, not to phone him back—he was turning in early. On Tuesday morning, she cringed at the ringtone, shrugging off her involuntary response. Once he finished filling her in on every little thing about his previous day's work, which caused her to stifle a yawn, she showed him a brief video of Chloe.

"What an ugly dog. I know I said you could get a rescue dog, and I meant a mutt, but boy is she ugly. Couldn't you do any better than her?"

Aurora's throat throbbed as she swallowed her desired response. She reached down and stroked Chloe's soft shaggy coat. "She's sweet, Jeff. She's lost a couple of toes. They think she was chasing a car and got her foot run over."

"A crippled dog on top of being ugly?"

"Don't be mean." He must have gotten up on the wrong side of the bed. She hated it when his attitude sucked.

"I don't think I'm being mean, just realistic. An injured, ugly dog. I bet she's sickly, and you want to make her well."

"She's not sickly. She's just missing some toes." Her face grew hot.

"Whew. I don't know about you sometimes, Aurora. But, changing the subject, did you tell me when our appointment with the lawyer is to do our wills? If you did, I forgot to put it in my calendar."

"Um, yeah, I was supposed to make that appointment. Right?"

"You forgot? Don't you remember anything? Other than I let you get a dog. After we had sex the other night, we discussed getting our wills made. We're supposed to be leaving everything to each other."

She preferred the term *making love* to *having sex*. After a faux laugh, she said, "Mmm. I was only kidding. I'm waiting for a call back. His assistant said he makes his own appointments, and he's in trial this week."

"You said you'd call him last Friday." His voice grew louder.

"I did. I called him Friday afternoon, but the office closes at noon on Fridays." She hoped he didn't remember she'd said she'd phone again on Monday.

Dead silence, and then, "Let me know as soon as you get an appointment set up."

"Yes, sir." She tried to put as much attitude in her voice as she thought would carry through to his end of the connection.

"Not funny, Aurora. What about an insurance agent? I bet you didn't call an insurance agent either."

She was glad he wasn't there and couldn't see her stick out her tongue. He acted like he was a lawyer, and she was on trial. "Was I supposed to do an insurance agent, too? *That* I really don't remember, but if I said I would, I will tomorrow." She didn't like that he was pressing her on those three things, especially the life insurance. What was the hurry?

"Damn, Aurora. You spend all your time writing a book you think you're going to get published and on the animals at the shelter. You don't have any consideration for me."

Her neck tightened, and a headache threatened. She wished he'd hang up. "That's not true, Jeff. Please don't say that. I've been working in the barn, too."

"Well, that's what it feels like. I guess I'd better go."

Had he read her mind? Just to annoy him, she asked, "Don't you want to hear about the latest news around here, about what's been going on?"

"You can fill me in when I get home, along with whatever the lawyer and insurance agent say once you finally get around to talking to them. Make appointments for us to meet them as soon as possible."

His habit of disconnecting without saying goodbye, irked her. "It's okay, Chloe. It's just you and me for another few days." She patted the dog's head. "We're good. And don't worry, you're not going anywhere." She put the phone down and went back to her computer and the book he said she *thought* she was going to get published. What a horrid comment. He must really be having a bad day. Well, phooey on him. She'd make those calls when she felt like it and no sooner.

A couple of hours later, someone knocked on the kitchen door. Aurora had been in the middle of what she considered a really important scene, so she didn't answer right away. She wrote a few more sentences in spite of the second knock. Finally, she saved her work. Her writing program was supposed to automatically save it, but Aurora didn't trust tech stuff. She found it hard to keep up with.

Ian stood on their small stoop. He wore jeans, an olive T-shirt with an unbuttoned denim long-sleeved shirt over it, work boots, and sunglasses, which he pushed up to the top of his head when she pulled the door open. His woodsy scent greeted her. Good thing Sarah wasn't around.

"Ian, what's up?" Chloe stood behind Aurora, her snout pushed up against Aurora's calf. Aurora reached down and trailed her fingers across the dog' back.

"Thought I might catch you working. I've thought of a couple of more things I think y'all might have out there."

"You did. I'm working on my novel. I may not have mentioned it, but one of my goals is to get a book published."

"What's it about? No, don't tell me. I've heard writers don't want to give away their story until they've finished. I see you have the dog, though."

"Chloe. You want to introduce yourself?" Aurora pulled the door wider.

Ian held his hand out for a few moments. Then he crouched down so he was face-to-face with Chloe, which Aurora thought Chloe wouldn't like, but she took a couple of steps toward Ian. He looked at the plastic cone around her neck and ran his eyes across her body until he came to Chloe's feet. "She's injured?" He stroked her forehead with one finger.

"They said her foot was probably run over while chasing a car."

"Awww, poor baby." He tickled her chest and smiled at her. "She's a sweetheart." He stood up. "You have a dog run already."

Aurora nodded. "Taylor had someone put it in for me. Said she had grant money."

"Right." One side of his mouth rose in a half smile. "Is Jeff here?" He glanced over her shoulder.

"Even if he was in town, Jeff wouldn't be home. He'd be around the county calling on hospitals. But he's on the road again."

"Like the song. Where's he off to this time?"

"I'm not sure. I didn't ask him again. If he said, I don't remember. I know I'm terrible about that. So, anyway, you want to go out to the barn? I'll put Chloe in the dog run. Did you bring your dog?"

"Yeah, but I'll leave him in the truck for now. He'll be okay. He can meet Chloe another time." Bending over, he said, "Nice meeting you, Chloe." He backed out of the doorway and down into the yard.

Aurora could swear Chloe grinned at him. After grabbing a thin jacket out of her closet, she put Chloe on a leash and took her outside. Opening the gate, Aurora urged the dog to go in and, when she did, removed the leash and closed the gate, hanging the leash on the fence.

Ian was busy digging through the junk still behind the yellow crime scene tape. Aurora had removed the windows but only made a dent in everything the day she'd found the knife. She remembered the knife about the same time Ian appeared to spot it stuck in the window she'd dragged aside.

"What's this?" Without touching anything, he examined the knife.

"I couldn't get it unstuck. I don't know why a knife would be stuck in a window, but whoever put it there must have shoved hard."

"That's a strange thing to find in your *barn*."

Aurora shrugged. "Not really. We've found several interesting things, including animal skulls."

"But a knife. And looks like blood could be on it."

"I thought it was probably rust. Anyway, when I tried to get it unstuck, I got some of whatever it is on my gloves and stupidly wiped them on my clothes and when I washed my clothes, it wouldn't come out. Rust would do that, right?"

"So would blood. Have you called the police?"

"Why would I? All this junk has been in here since before my grandfather died."

He stared down at her. "You sure?"

Aurora thought about the night she'd caught someone in the barn, the night she'd seen the light in the barn and gone to investigate. An acrid taste rose in the back of her throat. "Well..."

"What? Do you know otherwise?"

She wasn't sure she should tell Ian anything. She didn't really know him. He was just some man, albeit a friendly one, who flipped houses. They weren't friends or anything. But he did sound concerned. Her eyes raked over his face. Her rapid heartbeat drew her attention. Why was she nervous? If he was asking about the knife, it wasn't like he was threatening her or anything. While all that ran through her head, he continued to stare down at her.

"Okay, well, I haven't really shared this with anyone, but I'll tell you something, if you keep it to yourself."

"Have you found other things like this knife? Other things with blood on them?"

"We don't know it's blood, Ian. I still think it's rust."

"Only one way to find out. Have it tested. You can call the P.D. Anyway, what is it you haven't told anyone?"

She chewed on her lower lip. "You remember the first sale we had? The one where you came the first time?"

Ian nodded. He folded his arms across his chest and stood with his legs spread like she'd seen cops do on TV. The cops across the street stood like that, so did Dalton.

"Are you a police officer, Ian?" Sarah might think he was a serial killer, but he sure had the demeanor of a cop.

He looked startled. "Why do you ask?"

"Just the way you're standing over me. I feel like you're fixing to give me the third degree."

"No. Not a police officer." He dropped his arms and straightened up. "I'm sorry if I'm intimidating you." He stepped back. "I realize sometimes people are wary of me."

He was pretty big, but then she was used to big, Jeff being tall, too. "Dalton—that's–uh—the police officer who my friend Georgina, who is also a cop, is dating. He poses with his hands on his hips. He was here the other day—well, a couple of times, especially about the woman who was killed across the street."

"Someone died across the street?" He strode to the doorway. "The house over there? I just realized there's crime scene tape lying on the ground in front of the stoop."

"You hadn't heard? We figured it would be all over town by now. Yeah, this woman was found dead the other day."

"They think someone killed her?"

"From what I can find out. She'd been dead several days."

He cleared his throat. "And you're here all alone a lot of the time." He walked back to where she stood.

Aurora shivered. "But now I have Chloe. She'll bark if someone comes close."

"I didn't hear her bark when I came to your door."

"Oh, well. I think she'll get the hang of it once she realizes my house is her house. Isn't that what dogs do? They bark when they know someone is close to their home?"

"Ordinarily." He glanced toward the house across the street. Looking back at her, he asked, "What were you going to tell me before? About the knife?"

"Okay, well, there was someone in the barn the night before our sale. I thought it was probably kids and came out to run them off. Whoever it was ran away after knocking me down."

"You didn't see who it was? Did you call the police? What did Jeff say?"

She picked up a piece of a child-sized chair, white paint flaking off, and tossed it toward the door. "I didn't tell Jeff, at first. I didn't want him to worry about me when he's out of town. But then I finally told him, and that's why he said I could get Chloe. Well, not Chloe exactly, but a dog." She wasn't going to mention what Jeff said about Chloe.

She had her back to him, picking through a pile of wood, more pieces of chair backs and chair legs. He tapped her on the shoulder.

"Would you mind telling me what happened?"

Wishing she hadn't brought it up, she turned toward him. "Just someone rummaging around in here, that's all. I didn't want to make a big deal out of it."

"At night? Was it dark? How did you know he was in here?"

"I don't know if the person was a *he*, but probably so." She shrugged. "Okay. I was sleeping. Jeff was out of town, due back late, but it was the middle of the night. He wasn't home yet, otherwise I would have asked him to investigate when I saw the light. I got up to go to the bathroom and a light flashed in the bathroom window. The bathroom is at the back of the house, so I knew it wasn't car lights from someone driving past the vacant lot."

"And you came out here to see who it was?" His brows drew together.

"I was kinda annoyed someone would come to steal something when we'd be practically giving stuff away the next day. I thought it was probably just kids seeing what they could find. Anyway, I put on my robe and shoes and turned on my phone flashlight and came out here. I waved the phone around, hoping whoever it was would see my light and leave. Well, they did. They ran out fast, knocking me to the ground and leaping over the junk in the yard, and headed up the street there, up the slope." She pointed to the road leading up to Main Street.

"Wow. I guess you weren't hurt."

"Just a little scrape. I know you're going to ask me if I saw who it was, or can I describe them. The answer is no and no. He was wearing a dark hoodie."

"And you didn't think to call the police?"

She moved back. Her neck was starting to ache from looking up at him. "At two o'clock in the morning when I wasn't hurt and they didn't take anything as far as I could see? No. I brushed myself off and went back to bed."

"And didn't tell Jeff when he got home." His hands had gone to his hip in a lecturer's stance.

"I was asleep when he came to bed."

"You know what I mean."

"You were here when he got up Saturday morning. Remember when he came out with his coffee? But I've told him now, anyway."

"You're trying to be argumentative, Aurora. I'm just trying to get at the facts. I want to be sure you're going to be all right."

Now he sounded like a lawyer. "Why? You don't even know me." She couldn't fathom why he was so interested.

"You're right. But I wouldn't want to see anyone get hurt. I'd like you to inform Officer Dalton. I'd feel better if you did."

"Do you know Dalton?" Maybe Ian was concerned about the stuff he left lying around in the evenings after he quit working on his house. Someone could steal his supplies. Or maybe he'd already had an incident.

Ian shook his head. "I just think letting the police know would be the best thing. That's what I would do."

"Have you had an incident at your house?"

"Not yet. But now I wonder if it's just a matter of time. So, are you going to call?"

"I'll think about it." She had a dog now to alert her. Did she really need security in such a small town? She would think about it, maybe discuss it with Jeff, or not. She could maybe tell Georgina. She was a cop. Or Sarah, or not. Or her other friends, or not.

CHAPTER

FOURTEEN

Aurora pulled a load of clothes from the dryer and took them into the bedroom to fold while they were still warm. When she came to the pants she'd been wearing when she'd found the knife, the brown stain was still there. She'd run them through the washer twice. She dug around in the rest of the things from the dryer and found the dishcloth. The stain hadn't come out of it either. Bummer. The thought that the gunk had been blood, not rust, caused a twitch in her stomach. She wouldn't be wearing the pants again or using the dishrag on her dishes. She stuffed them in a plastic bag and put them in her suitcase at the top of the closet.

Before sunset, dressed in her ripped jeans and an old cotton sweater, Aurora grabbed the leash and clipped it onto Chloe's collar. Taylor had advised Aurora to train Chloe to heel. To do that, Aurora needed to start walking the dog. Chloe had been doing all right around the house and in the dog run with no difficulty. Fewer toes didn't appear to affect her gait. She ought to do well on pavement. And it was past time for Aurora to meet some neighbors, as well, even if they were probably out of shouting distance. She crouched down in front of the dog and, scratching her under the chin, said,

"Chloe, want to go for a walk?" Chloe wagged her tail and licked Aurora's face, giving off a strong whiff of kibble. Obviously, Chloe recognized both a leash and the word *walk*.

No sooner did Aurora lock the back door behind her and take a few steps toward the road than Chloe began tugging on the leash. She caught Aurora off balance, almost causing her to fall. Straightening up, Aurora got a better grip and pulled back. Taylor had told her to be tough with the dog and, of course, to reinforce any good behavior. Aurora had some snacks in her pocket to reward Chloe if she responded to commands.

"Heel!" Aurora said and pulled back until Chloe stopped and looked up at her with her pleading, puppy dog eyes.

Aurora winced. She didn't want to hurt Chloe. But Taylor's words came back to remind her. *She's a dog. You're a human. You have to train her to protect her.*

Aurora drew a deep breath and told herself to be strong. She began walking in her normal pace, holding the leash tight. Chloe did well until they reached the street. A car cruised by going toward the slope to town. Chloe jerked the leash out of Aurora's hand and bounded after the car.

"Chloe, no!" Aurora ran after the dog who, barking her head off, stopped at the back tire when the car slowed for the stop sign. Aurora was able to catch up and grab the leash again. "Bad girl!" She pulled on the leash until they stood on the vacant lot next to the house. Training Chloe was going to be harder than Aurora had imagined. At least she now knew the dog could bark.

Crouching down, Aurora frowned and said in a stern voice, "Bad Chloe. Bad."

Chloe cowered and hung her head. Feeling sorry, Aurora reached out to pet the dog then pulled her hand back. She realized petting her would give a conflicting message. She didn't want her dog to be killed by a car. Again, Taylor's words came back to her. *"She's a dog, not a person. You have to be firm. Don't reward her in any way for bad behavior."*

"Okay, girl, we're going to try this again." She gave the leash a little pull but had ratcheted up the length, so Chloe couldn't get far away. Walking slowly off the grass onto the street, Aurora spoke in a soft tone, hoping Chloe would learn to tune in to her voice.

The crime scene tape had begun to flap in the breeze at the house across the street. Aurora averted her eyes. She needed to focus on the issue at hand and not get distracted by the death of the woman a few yards from where she and Chloe stood.

A 60ish man strode toward them from the South end of the street. He wore a gimme cap and touched the bill. "Good afternoon. Training your dog?"

Aurora stopped in the street. "Yes, sir. I just got her. She's a rescue, and we're learning how to walk together."

"She's quite a mix, a Heinz 57."

Aurora laughed, but inside she was hoping the man wasn't going to insult Chloe, call her ugly like Jeff had. "I vaguely remember my grandparents using the Heinz 57 Sauce description. No one says that phrase much these days. At least I don't. I like to think of Chloe as a mosaic."

"Chloe, that's a good name for her." He didn't draw close but leaned down a bit and looked in Chloe's face. "I think she's smiling at me."

"She probably recognizes you like dogs."

"I do." He stepped away. "I'll be on my way. Enjoy your walk with your little girl."

"Oh, mister, what's your name, and where do you live? Are we neighbors?"

"Oh, sorry. Frank Brooks. I'm about two streets down, second house on the right."

"I'm Aurora Morris." She gestured behind herself. "This is my house."

"I know. I came to your sale, but there were so many people you probably didn't see me. I knew your grandparents." He waved and strode in the direction of Main Street.

Aurora turned back in the other direction, still holding the leash tight, and crept along. After a few steps, she stopped and said, "Heel," like Taylor had shown her.

Chloe stopped and looked up.

Aurora grinned and pulled a treat out of her pocket. Just one. "Good girl. Here's a reward."

Chloe took it, being careful of Aurora's fingers. Had the dog come from a loving home? If so, why was she found at that awful house?

They continued down the road, away from Main Street, for several blocks with Aurora stopping occasionally and ordering Chloe to heel. Chloe got it right several times though not always.

The houses were spaced far apart on the road running in front of Aurora's, and in each block, another street ran perpendicular and bore houses as well. All the lots were larger than what could be found in recent developments. Aurora and Chloe didn't come across any other people, just manicured lawns, trees, and porches decorated with pumpkins and chrysanthemums.

When they returned from their walk, she put Chloe out in the dog run with a big bowl of water and some more kibble. After chugging a big glass of water, Aurora texted Sarah and asked her to come over when she could. In the meantime, since it was late afternoon, she put together a salad with some thawed cooked shrimp and sat munching lettuce and spring greens out on the porch as the sun began its descent.

Just as it began to grow dark, Sarah drove up and bounced out of her vehicle and across the yard to where Aurora was just about to go inside and wash her salad bowl.

"Hiya!" Sarah called. She wore jeans, a pullover forest green hoodie, and tennis shoes.

"Hey, girl," Aurora said. "Come inside with me while I put this away and get a jacket since it's starting to get cool."

"What's up? Are we going somewhere?"

"Once it's really dark, we'll go across the street and see what we can see in the dead woman's windows."

"I'm game." Her eyes lit up with excitement. "Finally, we're going to see some action. In the meantime, got any wine?"

"Yep, and something I want to tell you." Aurora laid the washed salad bowl and utensils in the dish rack and dried her hands. "You know where the wine glasses are. I'll get the bottle."

Aurora grabbed a bottle of white wine from the refrigerator and put it on the table. "Want to open it while I get my jacket? And I'm going to let Chloe in."

"Sure." Sarah made herself at home. She opened the wine and poured herself a glass.

When Aurora brought Chloe in from the dog run, Sarah crouched down in front of the dog like they were old friends.

Aurora went to the bedroom for a light jacket and returned barefoot with boots in her hand. "In case there are weeds we have to trudge through," she said to Sarah's inquiring eyes, but didn't mention the possibility of snakes.

Chloe trotted over and licked Aurora's hand. "This dog is hungry a lot. I don't care what Taylor says, I'm going to give her lots to eat until she fattens up a bit and then do the morning and evening meal thing."

Sarah stared at her and cocked one shoulder. "Okay by me."

"I'm sorry. In my head I'm arguing my point. Did I tell you I showed Jeff a picture of Chloe, and he said mean things about her? I don't know what's wrong with him. He used to be the sweetest, most considerate, charmingist—is that a word?—human being around."

Sarah rubbed a knuckle across her lips and batted her eyes.

"I saw what you did. But he was sweet and charming. You didn't know him when we lived in Houston. Even when I lost the baby, he was so good about everything." Aurora dumped some dog food into a bowl she'd put out of the way of traffic and filled the water bowl with fresh water. Chloe tiptoed to her dishes and smiled at Aurora before beginning to eat.

"Maybe he's decided he doesn't want to live out here."

"That's what I'm afraid of. But I do, and I have no plans to leave."

She filled a glass with wine and sat in the kitchen chair opposite Sarah, determined not to share any of her haunting doubts about Jeff.

Sarah's eyebrows shot up. "That's showing some grit."

Aurora shrugged. "Anyway, I've got something else I need to tell you."

Sarah dry-washed her hands. "Something juicy, I hope."

"Not exactly." Aurora tossed back a gulp of wine and sputtered. After coughing for a few moments, she wiped her eyes, "went down the wrong way," and swallowed the rest. "C'mon it's dark. Drink up and grab your cell."

Sarah followed her lead and drained her own glass.

"Chloe stay," Aurora said in a firm voice. She slipped her cell into her back pocket.

"Does she know any commands yet?"

"She's learning." Aurora stalked to the back door and held it open for Sarah. "Let's go." She swept her hand in the air to indicate Sarah should depart first. Tapping on her cell phone light, Aurora stepped outside. She reached inside before closing the door and turned off the porch light so they couldn't be seen so easily.

Sarah turned on her own light and held it against her chest. "So, what's the news you said you'd share?"

Aurora took Sarah's arm as they walked to the drive. No cars came from either way, so they jogged across the street.

"Okay, the night before our first sale, someone, I guess you could say, burglarized the barn."

"What?" Sarah pulled her arm away. "And you didn't tell me?"

Aurora tugged on Sarah's sleeve. "Let's go around back. I was sleeping and got up to pee. When I went into the bathroom, a light flashed the window."

The dead woman's house was a pier and beam and, consequently, raised off the ground several feet with a lattice skirt around the bottom. Luckily, there were tall, wood-framed windows, the old-fashioned kind with squares of glass coming down almost to the floor.

"Here comes a car," Sarah said, pressing her phone against her leg so the light wouldn't be seen and pulling Aurora to the side of the house. Aurora hid her light, as well. Sarah stopped and confronted Aurora. "Someone was in your barn the night before the sale? I can't believe you didn't tell us. What happened?"

Aurora stood on tiptoes and flashed her cell phone light into the first window. The outside of the window was dirty, so she wiped away a circle of dirt with her fingers. "Can't really see anything. You want to look? You're taller."

"I want you to tell me what happened," Sarah said, but she wiped a bigger space with her own fingers and shone her light inside. "I see a table and chairs. Like a dinette set."

"Let's go to the next window."

Sarah took Aurora's arm. "First, tell me what happened. I'm sounding like a recording, but you can't say you have something to tell me and then drag it out like this. I'm going nuts waiting ..."

Aurora gave the rundown of what happened to Sarah who stood open-mouthed.

"Oh my God, Aurora. I guess you weren't hurt? But you couldn't have called the police, or we'd already know about it. Did you tell Jeff? What did the person look like? What did Jeff say when you told him?"

Aurora reached the second window and rubbed a circle in the dirt again, a bigger circle. Shining her light in, she could just see the bottom of a stripped bed and some table legs.

"You're so casual about this. So nonchalant. Would you please answer me?"

Aurora turned to Sarah. "Okay. I didn't see who it was, but I think it was a man. He wore a dark—I think it was probably black—hoodie and dark pants. I didn't tell Jeff until recently, and that's why he let me get a dog. I told Ian, and he told me I needed to tell the police. Do you think I should?"

"You talked to Ian? He was here again? Aren't you worried, being alone when he comes by?"

"Don't get distracted, Sarah. It does a little, but he never appears threatening. He's stopped by here several times during the day to look over stuff for his house."

"You're not afraid?"

"If he was going to hurt me, don't you think he would have done it already? You're so suspicious."

"We've talked about this. He came out of nowhere right about the time they started finding dead women in this part of the county."

"He didn't come out of nowhere. We just didn't know him. He's been working on his house."

"Do we really know he's telling the truth? Maybe he just bought it and is using the story of fixing it up to hide himself, to give him a reason for being here."

"You're so distrustful. I don't think so, Sarah, anyway, I did tell him."

"Why did you tell him and not us, your friends?"

Aurora chewed her lip. "I'm trying to think. Why did I tell him? Oh, because of the knife."

"There was a knife?" Sarah jerked on Aurora's forearm. "What knife?"

Aurora wrestled her arm back. "Quit grabbing my arm. I found a knife in the barn stuck in the frame of one of the windows in the never-ending-pile. Which is now nonexistent I'm happy to say. Anyway, I couldn't get it out."

Sarah's face drew together in a huge frown. "What the heck? Sometimes I think I don't know you. You found a knife in your barn after someone was in your barn and a woman turned up dead across the street. Have I got that right?"

"You don't have to get so weird about it."

"You don't think *you're* the one being weird? Why haven't you told the police?"

"The night in the barn, I didn't think was significant. I thought it was some kid. Then we had the sale and all, and I forgot about it." She moved around to the back of the house, which smelled like mildew. Her eyes burned.

Sarah shone her light into the second window and followed Aurora really close. When Aurora stopped, Sarah bumped into her.

"When they found a dead woman in here, it kind of creeped me out, but I didn't see how it could be related. Now I'm thinking maybe it is." Aurora stomped on some tall weeds, crushing them so they could walk over them. The back windows were higher than the ones on the side of the house.

"Because ..."

Aurora turned to her. "Because Ian thought what I thought were rust stains on the knife were blood stains and could have been fresh, even though dry, on the knife."

"I think I understand. Was the dead woman in this house stabbed? Was the knife you found, *the* knife?"

"We don't know, but maybe Georgina will tell us. Anyway, I told Jeff about someone in the barn and let him know I was a little alarmed."

"No kidding. No wonder Jeff let you get a dog. What else did he say?"

"Who, Jeff?"

"No, Ian." Sarah, being taller than Aurora, stood on her tiptoes and looked into the back window. "There's not much to this house. This is a wide room, a washroom, with an older model washer and dryer. I thought we might be able to see where she died, but there's nothing to see."

"Ian asked if I'd told Dalton."

"With everything that's going on, with those women being killed and this woman being dead," Sarah said, "I would tell Dalton even though the cops might not think this was related to the others. And Georgina. She needs to know. In fact, if it was me, I'd get an alarm system and new locks. I'd be scared to death to be out here alone."

"We have new locks now, and it's not *out here*, Sarah. There are houses all around, cars driving up and down the street. In fact, I met a neighbor man when I was walking Chloe."

"Well, that's good. Where does he live?"

"A couple of streets down, but at least I finally met someone."

"He won't be any help. These old houses are on huge lots and are kind of far apart on this side of town. Something could happen to you, and no one would hear it. Like what happened to this woman."

Aurora shivered. "I didn't tell you the rest of it." They rounded the back of the house. "The knife was jammed between the glass and the frame in one of the windows in the pile in the back of the barn."

"Oh my God, Aurora. You think the person who was in the barn shoved the knife there? He was hiding it after he killed this lady?" She shivered, too. "I have goose bumps."

"I was wondering why he stuck it in a window frame. He could have thrown it in the bayou. Anyway, I think that's why Ian asked me if I was going to tell Dalton."

"Did he think whoever it was might come back for the knife?"

"I don't know what he was thinking, but surely whoever it was wouldn't come back after several weeks. He's had plenty of time. You think I should tell Dalton?"

"Uh, yeah. Don't you? Is the knife still there?"

They'd peered through two more windows on the other side the little house and reached the crime scene tape, one end blowing in the breeze, the other still tied to a porch railing. "Why did I want to come over here? There's nothing here."

"Must have seemed like a good idea at the time," Sarah said with a forced laugh. "You didn't answer me. Is the knife still there?"

Aurora nodded. "Ian didn't touch it. He just told me to call Dalton. Let's go back."

"That's so weird. A knife just sticking out of a window in your barn. This is so creepy. Want me to stay with you tonight?"

Aurora shook her head. "There have been a lot of nights since then, Sarah. So, no. But there was one more thing I wanted to tell you. The night I saw the light in the barn, I was having some kind of bad dream before I woke up to go pee. In my dream someone screamed. I woke up." She took her lower lip between her teeth for a moment. "More and more I think maybe she screamed when she was murdered. Just think, if it was the murderer in my barn, he only knocked me down when he could have killed me."

"With it being in the middle of the night and you being all alone, I wonder why he didn't."

CHAPTER
FIFTEEN

I n the middle of what Aurora thought was the best chapter she'd written so far, someone banged on the door again. God, she was getting so tired of that. Chloe jumped up and ran out of the room, barking all the way. Someone stood outside the front door, not the back, which was the door everyone seemed to have gotten used to coming through. The front door had a large rectangular clear glass pane in it, which Aurora had somewhat covered with a thin gauzy curtain, but she could still see the uniform of the person standing on her front porch. She had an idea who it was.

When she pushed the curtain aside, Officer Dalton's steely eyes stared at her from the other side, his brow furrowed and his mouth in a stern line. Adrenaline spiked through her body. She pulled the door open.

"Good afternoon, officer," she said. She wore an old T-shirt and jeans again and glanced down at herself to see whether she was presentable since she had a bad habit of eating on her lap and spilling food on whatever she wore. The T-shirt only had one stain on it, a dark drip of something. Just once she wished she was wearing something decent when someone stopped by but not enough to actually change what she wore around the house.

Chloe had stopped barking and stood behind her, skittish but not threatening. Her nose bumped the back of Aurora's leg.

"Mrs. Morris," he said as he stood in the standard cop stance, legs spread, hands hovering just above his gun belt. "We received a report last night of two people at the house across the street, moving around the house and looking in the windows."

"Oh, yeah?" She didn't know who could have called it in. She and Sarah hadn't seen anyone, but they hadn't been making a huge effort to hide. They'd figured it being dark, probably no one would have seen them with the houses so far apart, as Sarah had mentioned. "You want to come in?" She took Chloe by the collar and backed up so he could enter.

The little house had a combined kitchen and dining room and not much of them, though her grandparents had always found it adequate. When she was small, the space felt a lot larger. An antique, dark oak table and four wooden chairs stood in the dining room part. Dalton came in and closed the door behind himself, bringing a musky masculine scent with him. He pulled out a chair to sit after she did.

"Sit, Chloe," she said and patted her rump, pleased when Chloe sat next to her chair.

"I'm glad you came by, officer. I have something I guess I need to tell you."

He held his palm out to stop her. "Let me get to what I came here for, first."

Aurora had hoped they could skip to his reason for showing up and go straight to the person in the barn and the discovery of the knife. "Okay, go ahead."

"You and one of your and Georgina's women friends were seen peeking in the windows of the house across the street last night. I don't know who your associate was, but I know it wasn't Georgina. We were together."

"I knew y'all were dating. She told us." Aurora gave him her best smile.

"Mrs. Morris, I need you to answer my question."

"Aurora. Call me Aurora. We weren't doing anything except looking in the windows to see what was there. We aren't in any trouble, are we? We didn't do anything else."

"Trespassing."

Aurora's body tensed. "The owner isn't around to file anything."

He cocked one eyebrow. "I'm not here to argue with you. The two of you were trespassing. You know you were. You've seen the crime scene tape. I just want to advise you not to do it again."

"There's nothing there anyway," Aurora said, refraining from rapid blinking.

"There could be evidence from the murder, some evidence not found the first time." He started to rise. "So just restrain yourselves." He gave her the dark eye.

"So, it was a murder." He had just confirmed what she already knew. "Don't leave. I have something to tell you." Her stomach began acting up again.

He eased back into the chair. "Is this an official report?"

"Y—yes, it is. I probably should have reported it sooner. But anyhoo, you probably know we've been selling my grandfather's uh —clutter—including having a sale a few weekends ago. Georgina was here. You probably know about it."

"I do. Something happen then?"

"No, not then." She told him about the incident from the night before the sale, describing what she knew of the intruder.

"Were you assaulted?"

"Not really, just knocked down. Not hurt or anything, just scared for a few minutes."

"And you have no idea who it was."

"I thought it was probably a kid trying to see what he could steal, then I found the knife."

He reared back. "A knife. What kind of knife?"

145

For some reason, she found his reaction funny but held in a chuckle. Holding her forefingers about six or so inches apart. "'Bout yay long."

"No. I mean pocketknife, kitchen knife—"

"Do you want to see it?"

"You still have it?"

"It's stuck in a window in the barn. I'll show you, but let me put Chloe out in the dog run first." As Aurora led him out the back door, she was grateful there was something to take his attention from the trespass of the night before. Made him friendlier.

"Just so you know, Mrs. Morris, I haven't forgotten about the reason I came here, but I'm going to let you off with a warning. I don't know which one of your friends was over there with you last night, but don't do it again and tell her the same."

"Yes, sir," she said without turning around. She wanted to say he'd already warned her once, but she didn't want to get on his bad side any worse than she already was.

When they entered the barn, she indicated the double-hung window she had placed near the door. He strode toward it. "Have you touched this?"

"Well, yeah. I tried to pull it out, but it's stuck."

"When did you find it?"

"Only a few days ago. A woman wants to buy all the old windows, so I've been digging through this junk to pull them out for her. I couldn't get the knife out even with my gloves on or a rag I got from the kitchen."

He mumbled. "Any fingerprints would be long gone."

"You don't think it's connected to the woman across the street, do you? Ian said he thought that's blood on the knife. I thought it was rust. But if it's blood, could it be related to her? Was she stabbed or something?"

A muscle in his jaw flexed. He stood with his hands on his hips. "I can't discuss the details with you."

If he wasn't going to tell her anything, then she wasn't going to give him the knife, assuming he wanted it. "Okay, then, I just thought I'd show it to you." She took a couple of steps toward the yard.

He didn't move. "I'm going to have someone come pull it out and take it to the lab. There appears to be some kind of substance still close to the blade."

"You think it's connected? I didn't think it was important or anything, but when Ian asked me if I was going to call the police, I thought I should."

"Ian? That's the second time you've mentioned whoever he is."

"He's this man who has been buying some of this stuff for a house he's fixing up. Do you know him?"

His face showed a flicker of interest, which quickly shifted back to his normal poker face. "I think I've driven past his house when I've been on patrol."

She wondered whether there was any police interest in Ian, whether Georgina had told him what they'd discussed. What Sarah had said about him fixing up houses and moving on to the next town like a serial killer could do for cover. Seemed silly, really, but they had also discussed how something didn't ring true about Ian.

"I know you're not supposed to tell me, but is there anything I need to know about what happened across the street? Should I be worried? I guess you're thinking she was killed with the knife? Stabbed or someone cut her throat."

"That's awfully graphic."

She shrugged. "I'm writing a book. It was going to be a who-dun-it mystery at first, but I'm thinking now if someone died by murder across the street, maybe I should make it into a ..." She started to say serial killer mystery but hesitated long enough for him to lose interest.

"Whatever." He shook his head and looked around the barn. "Y'all still have a lot of stuff to unload."

"I'm getting tired of holding sales and thinking of asking my husband if it's okay for me to hire someone to haul everything off."

"Any reason for you to think there might be something else of interest in here?"

"Not really. I mean, I didn't expect to find a knife."

"Of course not. You have any idea how long the person you saw was actually in the barn?"

"Not really," she said again. "I went to the bathroom and saw the light and a few minutes later I came out here, so only maybe five minutes went by. He could have been in here for a while. I wouldn't have known."

"The next morning, you didn't see anything disturbed? Anything he might have moved for some reason?"

She waved her hand across the width of the barn. "As if I would have noticed. Naw."

"And you have no reason to think he might come back for the knife?"

She shivered. "That's a creepy thought, but he's had plenty of time if he wanted to."

He nodded. "Okay, well, as I said, I'll ask someone to come out to get the knife. Don't try to take it out again yourself." He moved toward the yard.

"I won't. Can I ask you something else?" The walked toward the street.

"Sure."

"I don't know if Georgina has told you, and you might think it's silly, but she and I and our other friends have been talking about those women who keep being found dead all around Harris and Galveston County."

"Yeah, and ..."

"So, figuring it's a serial killer, that being the obvious thing that's going on, is there any reason for y'all, the police around here in the 'burbs, to think the person lives in this neck of the woods?" She hesitated to say Ian's name, because she didn't want to get him into trouble, but on the other hand, if it was him, the police needed to keep an eye on him.

He stopped and stared down at her. "I wish I could tell you we have an idea where the person lives. If we did, we'd have an idea of who he is."

"Makes sense. It's just um, Ian, I mean he seems nice and all, and he's come by here several times when I've been alone, and he hasn't done anything to me, but, and you're probably going to think this is crazy, but he moves around a lot. He flips houses in different towns. Wouldn't flipping houses and moving on be a good occupation for a serial killer? That's what we've been thinking."

"Georgina told me." His mouth turned down in a deep frown. "Though I don't think she mentioned he comes to your house. Why has he been here?"

"To buy some of our junk. You might not realize it, but some of Grandpa's stuff back there is at least a little valuable. When people were tearing down some of the old houses around here, or at least re-doing them, my grandfather was the one to clean up the sites. Besides the windows and doors, there are some antique pieces of trim and molding." Uh-oh, if Ian was at the point where he was putting up trim, he must be getting close to finishing the house, which meant he must be getting ready to leave town. They needed to figure out who he was and if he was the one.

"You think Ian whatever his name is—"

"Rawlings. I went to look him up on the Internet but couldn't find anything."

"Ian Rawlings. I'll try to remember his name. Other than what he does to make a living, is there any reason to believe he's dangerous? You said he comes by when you're alone. I take it you mean when your husband is out of town?"

"Yes. That's strange, isn't it? But then Jeff's out of town a lot. If the man was going to do something to me, I guess he would have done it already. But still ... there's something not quite right about him."

"Like what?"

"It's just a feeling I have. He always asks if Jeff is home, or where Jeff is, like he wants to be sure when I'll be alone."

"I don't think you have anything to worry about. Like you said, he's had plenty of chances to do something to you. But if it makes you feel better, I'll be sure to drive by here and his house more often, and I'll run a check on him and see what I can find out."

"I would feel a lot better, Officer Dalton, if you would circle by here occasionally."

He said, "How about you call me Quince, but only when I'm not here on official business."

"Which you are now, but anyway ... if I see you somewhere socially, I will." She stuck out her hand. "And I promise I won't go back across the street. If you can find your way to telling me after the stuff on the knife is tested whether or not it was my neighbor's blood on it—or anyone's blood on it—I would like to know."

"Deal. I probably shouldn't, but I will." He shook her hand. "You take care."

Dalton walked back to his police unit and left as Aurora stood watching. She got Chloe out of the dog run and took her back into the house.

The more Aurora thought of it, the more she thought Ian must be getting ready to leave town if he was putting finishing touches on his house. They'd better find out who he really was before it was too late, and he got away.

CHAPTER
SIXTEEN

Aurora filled Chloe's bowl and water dish before heading to the shower. Talking to Dalton about everything gave her the creeps and made her want to scrub all over. Afterward, she put on pajamas and a robe. She stuck her feet into her warmest house shoes and headed to the kitchen to have a bag of salad for dinner.

Sarah called when Aurora was in the middle of her meal. "Have you seen the newspaper?"

"Hello to you, too, Sarah." Aurora set down her fork. She'd put too much sweet dressing on her salad and was sick of it anyway.

"There's an article—well, not an article, but an obituary—you need to see in the Houston Chronicle."

"I don't get the paper. Why don't you read it to me?" She swallowed from her glass of wine, found it too sweet also, and, after setting her glass down, stroked Chloe's head. Chloe had become like her shadow, never far from her.

"You can subscribe online. Anyway, I'll summarize. The woman who died across the street from you worked at a private detective agency!"

"No way!" Heartburn attacked. An acrid taste rose in the back of her throat. Again, she was reminded to make an appointment with her pcp to find out whether she had acid reflux, or the stress of being married to Jeff—heck, her whole life in the past year—was just giving her a never-ending case of indigestion.

"Yes way, girlfriend! The obituary cites the day she died, where, and then, after accolades, states she had been employed as an investigator for the last ten years and names the agency."

"Well, how can you tell it was her? And, by the way, do you read the obits every day?"

"First, yes, I do. My grandmother used to live with us when I was little, and my mother would tease her, saying Grannie looked in the newspaper obituaries every day to see if she was still alive."

Aurora chuckled. "Okay, well, I don't subscribe to the paper even online. I read everything on YouTube. I do receive the freebie that's mostly ads with only a few articles in it. Certainly, no reports about who died."

"Yeah, well, anyway, I could tell by the date and the town, surprised anything from out here would be in the paper. Of course, her agency probably put it in the paper."

Aurora cleared her throat. She needed to pop a couple of antacids. "You've kind of gotten off topic."

"I know it was her, even though we never heard her name."

"Why don't you call Georgina? I bet she'd know for sure. She'd be off by now. Also, by the way, Quincy Dalton stopped by. You and I were seen last night."

Sarah howled with laughter. "What'd he say?"

"Glad you think that's funny. He didn't come to your house. Anyway, he said for us not to do it again. But I talked to him about Ian. I told him what we thought—what you think... He probably thinks we're being stupid, but he's going to run a check on him."

"That's good. You know I think Ian is drop dead gorgeous—"

"Maybe a term you shouldn't bandy around."

"Ha. Ha. Just think about it, though. Someone like Ian could easily lure a woman into going with him, or whatever. I mean, if you met him someplace, you'd be tempted, wouldn't you? I would."

"Well, I have Jeff." The memory of how they had met surfaced in her mind. In a bookstore. In the mall.

Sarah snorted. "Jeff's big and cute but has nothing on Ian. There's something about him. Ian, I mean, not Jeff."

"I've thought about the last time he came over and looked only for pieces of trim, maybe he's finishing his house and fixing to leave to go to another town." She pushed the memory of her meeting Jeff away. "I was just thinking if that's the case, Ian'll have to sand the pieces and paint them."

"How long would that take? LOL. He could be planning his escape. Are you thinking what I am? We have to find out if it's him before he gets away."

"Okay, well, start by calling Georgina and seeing if she knows about my neighbor being a detective. Oh, and maybe she's heard some other stuff we don't know about."

"Are you thinking if Ian's getting ready to move, he might have already found, or might still find, another victim before he leaves?"

"I don't know what I'm thinking, except if the dead woman was an investigator, wouldn't she have checked in with the police when she came to town? Wouldn't they know what she was doing here?"

"You would think so."

"Maybe she told them who she was investigating. What if it was Ian? What if she's been following him from town-to-town and he was onto her and he killed her and he stashed his knife in my barn, and I almost caught him—"

"Hey, Aurora, you're not writing a book here. Don't get carried away. I'm hanging up now and calling Georgina."

"But aren't you thinking the same thing?"

Sarah cleared her throat. "Okay, yes. I have chills. I'm really going to call Georgina now." She disconnected.

An hour later, Aurora was at her computer and on the phone with Jeff when someone banged nonstop on her back door. Barking her head off, Chloe jumped up and ran out of out of the room. "I have to go. TTYL, okay?"

"What's going on? Is your dog barking? I haven't finished telling you everything. Just see who it is and come back."

"Someone's at the door. It's probably Sarah. I can call you later."

"Just forget it. We can talk tomorrow." The line went dead.

Aurora looked at her phone and shook her head. What a grouch. She jogged to the other room, pulling Chloe back by the collar, and opening the door. Sarah and Georgina stood together like Siamese twins, both dressed in white sports-team T-shirts, jeans, and wind-breakers. It still hadn't rained in weeks, but a front had come in and caused the temperature to drop enough to need more than one layer. "What?" Aurora said in a loud voice.

"Can we come in? We have something to tell you."

Sarah, her breath giving off the aroma of fermented apples, pushed past Aurora and patted Chloe on the head. Georgina followed suit, though she crouched down and scratched Chloe under the chin and on her chest.

"Well, don't let me stop you," Aurora said, shutting the door behind them. "What's the big emergency?"

"Let's go sit down." Sarah led the way to Aurora's oak table in the dining room. Breathing hard, she threw herself into a chair.

Both Georgina and Aurora sat as well. Aurora crossed her arms. She was still getting accustomed to people dropping by without notice. Lately people seemed to think it was okay anytime, like a perpetual open house.

Georgina, scraping her lower lip with her teeth, said, "Sarah made me come over here. I blabbed something I probably shouldn't have, and now she's making me tell you."

"Making you. Ha. You're the one with the gun," Sarah said. "But it's important. Has to do with Ian. Go ahead. Tell her."

Georgina cut her eyes at Sarah. "There's a woman who got away from a man who kidnapped her."

The hair rose on Aurora's arms. She wasn't expecting that.

"And it sounds like Ian," Sarah said.

"Who was she? Do we know her?" Aurora blinked rapidly, her eyes tearing as she looked from one woman to the other.

"She was from Galveston." Georgina's hands shook. "I'm probably going to get into trouble for telling you this."

"Hang on, you two. Slow down. You want a glass of wine? I was just on the phone with Jeff and was going to have a glass of wine when I got off."

Sarah said, "I'm surprised you weren't going to have anything stronger."

"Stop, Sarah. We all know you don't like him. Y'all want some or not?" She went to the cupboard and took out some glasses. "All I have is white."

"I'll take a glass," Sarah said, not looking the least remorseful about what she'd said. "It might not go with what I've already had, but I could use something."

"Okay," Georgina said. She put her hands between her thighs as if trying to warm them. "I could use something, too. I'm not on duty."

Aurora pulled a three-quarters full bottle out of the refrigerator and twisted off the cap. After pouring some into each glass, she took one to each woman. Georgina's hands still shook when she took hers from Aurora.

Once they'd all had a sip, Aurora said, looking at Georgina, "So, why are you going to get into trouble?"

She took another sip. "I shouldn't have told Sarah this, but she called me just after I got off work." She breathed deeply and let it out. "Quince, being on the night shift, is going to keep me posted with what else he finds out. He had to work extra because of the investigation into this woman, who says she was almost killed by a man in a white truck."

Gooseflesh ran across Aurora's neck and down her back. How many times had she been alone with Ian? She shook her head, not wanting to believe what she was hearing. "Dalton was here this afternoon and didn't say anything about it."

"He wouldn't even if he knew already, which he didn't. When he returned to the station, he heard about it."

Sarah said, "You're not telling her what all you know."

Georgina gave Sarah the side eye again. "I'm getting to it. We got a call from a woman who said she wanted to talk to someone about a woman she and her husband had taken in when they found her collapsed across the street from their house, at the edge of a field."

"They sent you out there?" Aurora took a sip but had a hard time swallowing. Her throat was trying to close.

"Yeah. They called the ambulance first and when I arrived, the woman had been taken to the hospital."

Sarah cleared her throat. "Tell her the rest."

Georgina frowned bigly. "I am. After I spoke with them, I went to the hospital. The woman was still in the ER, but I waited and was able to talk to her."

"And, and ..." Sarah said.

"God, Sarah, hold your horses." Georgina took another sip of her wine. "The woman is from Galveston. She met this man at the mall. He was really nice and offered to help her carry out her purchases, and as she was closing the back of her SUV, he knocked her out. Next thing she knew, she was in a truck, and he was choking her."

Aurora's vision blurred and heat flashed through her body. Saliva poured into her mouth as she grabbed her stomach and put her head between her knees. "Oh my God," she uttered. "How'd she get away?"

"Are you all right?" Sarah crouched down in front of Aurora.

"I think I'm going to be sick." She gagged.

Sarah turned to Georgina. "Ian Rawlings has been here several times when she's been alone." She hurried to the sink and wet some paper towels.

"I'm sorry. I shouldn't have told you," Georgina said. "I didn't mean to frighten you." She rubbed Aurora's back. "Breathe deeply."

Aurora rocked forward and back, her head still down. Sarah

pushed the wet paper towels toward her. "Put these on your forehead. I'll get some more for your neck."

"I don't know what's wrong with me," Aurora said to the floor. She drew a deep breath. She didn't want to admit to herself what she was thinking, much less tell them.

Sarah pushed Aurora's hair aside and placed the paper towels across the back of her neck. "You're scared," Sarah hissed.

"I'm not ready to die," Aurora whispered.

"You're not going to die," Sarah said, leaning over her. "Everyone knows Ian's been over here several times. At least some of us do, anyway."

Georgina began pacing. "Maybe I shouldn't tell you the rest of it. I'm sorry I said anything."

Aurora said, "No. No. I want to know about it. Give me a moment." She breathed in and out a few more times and sat up. Perspiration had soaked her shirt. She wiped her forehead and watery eyes with the paper towels and handed them back to Sarah. "Okay, Georgina." Aurora let go with a big sigh. "I think I'm going to be all right. Tell me the rest."

"If you're sure ..." Her eyes swept Aurora's face, "Okay. He would choke her and then let go, and she'd kinda get back to her senses, and he'd choke her some more. Several times. Then he told her to get out of the truck and run."

"And remember one of the women they found before had tire tracks on her back?" Sarah added.

Aurora glanced from one friend to the other. "So, somehow she was able to run into a field or what?"

"That's the surprising thing, except it isn't," Georgina said.

"What? What does that even mean?"

"She was able to climb over the wire fence before he could get out of his truck. He didn't follow her."

"Couldn't he have just rammed the fence and gotten to her?" Aurora asked.

"I'd think he probably was afraid the wire would damage his truck," Georgina said with a glance at Sarah.

"It's razor wire," Sarah said. "It could have scratched his paint job, right? That stuff's tough. Sharp."

"It's horrible," Georgina said. "I wish it had never been invented."

"The governor has had his people stretch razor wire across the Rio Grande, so undocumented immigrants can't cross over. Isn't that what some people have been caught up on and drowned?"

Georgina nodded. "Nasty stuff."

"What all did she tell you? Could she describe him, the man?" Aurora asked.

"Well, her memory is foggy just now. She might remember more later, but he was really good-looking and tall. She said he must have been nice, or she wouldn't have let him walk out to the parking lot with her. She doesn't really remember leaving the mall."

"But he was driving a truck? A white truck?"

"Yeah, she said it was dirty. Muddy, kind of."

The gooseflesh rose on Aurora's arms again. Ian's truck always seemed to be dirty. Dang, it was muddy when he'd been there. "Oh, man. Ian's truck had mud on it when he came by."

"Well," Georgina said, "they're going to try to get tire imprints, and if they do, they could check Ian's tires, so that'll help."

"How are they going to get imprints of a tire when it's been so dry? I wish it would have rained," Aurora said, squeezing her eyes closed tight, hoping to ease the burning.

"We think Ian's moving soon," Sarah said. "He keeps coming by here and getting small pieces of wood to use as trim on his house."

Georgina looked at Aurora. "He's been by here more than at your garage—barn sales? I didn't understand that."

Nodding, Aurora said, "Several times. I told Dalton, and he said he'd check him out."

"If Quince comes by, don't tell him I told you all this stuff."

"He knows we've been worried, though," Sarah said.

"Just don't say anything, please."

"I won't. I promise," Aurora said. "Who am I going tell, anyway? Y'all or Jeff?"

Sarah said, "Well the others. We'll see them next Monday."

"It's probably not that guy Ian. Just because he drives a white truck," Georgina said and drained her wine glass, "doesn't mean anything."

"So does Jeff. So do a lot of people in Texas. Millions." Aurora was not liking this. Her friends all had guns, but she didn't. All she had was Chloe.

"I know, but still ..." Sarah said. "The poor woman. I was just thinking. She must be a fast runner to outrun a truck."

"She's a jogger, she said." Georgina stood and looked from one woman to the other. "She made it to the far side, across the street from the people who found her, and collapsed. When they found her, she was holding on to the bottom wire, her hand kind of stuck on the barb thingies."

"Her hands had to be sliced up and bleeding like crazy."

"Her hands were, and she had some cuts on her arms and body. Her clothes hung in strips." Georgina shuddered. "Anyway, I need to go. I know it's late in the day, but I have a nail appointment." She pointed at each of them. "Really don't tell a soul. I could lose my job."

"We won't," Aurora said. "I won't even tell Jeff, I promise."

"Georgina, thanks for following me over here to tell Aurora. I feel stupid, but I felt all jittery when you told me. I wanted her to know but felt like something would be lost in the translation if I tried to tell her about it."

Georgina gave each of them a brief hug and patted Chloe again before leaving. "Keep your doors locked, girls."

CHAPTER
SEVENTEEN

"When you hear something else, call one of us," Sarah hollered at Georgina's back. She and Aurora had stepped out on the back stoop. "We need to know what's going on!"

Georgina waved a hand in the air and kept walking.

Aurora closed the back door, and said, "Just because Ian is fixing up a house and going to move on to his next project soon doesn't mean he's killed anyone. Besides, he can't leave yet, he does have to paint."

"Are talking to me or yourself?" Sarah asked.

Aurora said, "Are we just being silly?" She opened the refrigerator door and stuck her head in, looking for something to munch on. "Want some cheese? I have an apple, too." She needed some food to distract her.

"Okay." Sarah plopped back into a chair. "Do *you* think we're being stupid? I wish I'd never said what I said the day of your first sale. But still ..."

Aurora retrieved the cheese and apple from the fridge and a knife and a cutting board and took it all to the table. "Pour us another glass of wine while I slice this."

Sarah rubbed her forehead. "Maybe he is. Maybe he isn't. But what if he is?"

"You're going to drive me nuts. What if he isn't? Is it fair to Ian to even mention him to Dalton?"

"You already did, and what if he is? Okay, what do we really know about him? And what about the person in your barn?" Sarah got another knife and cut herself a hunk of apple. "I like these crisp ones you've been buying."

"Gala. All right. Let's talk about this." Aurora offered the small cutting board to Sarah. "Have a slice of cheese." She pushed the napkin holder at her. "Here's what we know. A strange man comes to town. He buys a house and refurbishes, or whatever, it. He sells it and moves on to another town."

Sarah held the cheese up to her nose. "This is the good stuff. Yum."

"Glad you approve." She bit off a slice of cheese she'd speared with the knife.

"We can't find out anything about him on the Internet anywhere," Sarah said.

"A lot of people aren't on social media."

"But we found nothing, nada, zilch, anywhere. That's weird. And remember how mad he got when I said what I said?" She stuffed a piece of cheese into her mouth.

"Come on, Sarah, wouldn't you get mad if someone you just met accused you of being a serial killer?"

Sarah swallowed and said, "I didn't exactly accuse him. I was just saying—"

"I remember what you said. So, anyway, what else do we know about him? He has a dog and a white truck, and he's never even felt threatening to me when he comes over here. I hate to think anyone with a dog as sweet as Gerhard killed someone."

Shaking her head, Sarah said, "Ted Bundy was supposedly charming and well-spoken."

Aurora crossed her arms. "Yeah, right. But he was before we were even born."

"Still ... you hear about serial killers all the time."

"Sure, if you're watching crime shows on TV, Sarah, which I'm not. But you probably are." And the news, which Aurora thought but didn't say.

"Anyway, what else do we know? Nothing? And then there's the person in your barn and the knife." Sarah nibbled on another slice of apple. "What did you see? A black hoodie and someone you thought was probably a man. I have an idea though, if you want to hear it. We never have figured out what he does at night."

"Ian? Are you thinking again about trying to follow him?"

"No time like the present, but he may know my car by now," Sarah said.

Aurora knew Sarah had taken to driving past Ian's house more times than she'd let on. She'd even stopped once supposedly just to say hi. "I don't know. What if he sees us, recognizes us? In fact, what if he sees us, and he's the killer?"

"He wouldn't do anything. We have cell phones," Sarah said.

"He wouldn't do anything *tonight*. What about after we get to our homes, and we're alone?"

"He knows both of our cars, but if we use someone else's he won't know it's us. Maybe Monica will loan us her car."

"That's a possibility. Monica came by the other day when he was here, but she parked down the street. I don't think he came out of the garage the whole time she was here, or when she left." Aurora tapped her lips. "And he was here on the first Saturday when the others were here. He might know who goes to what car if we borrowed someone else's."

"Or he might not. Let's go with Monica. She lives not far from your house."

"Call her if you want. We'll see what she says. I'm still not so sure." Aurora's stomach started its churning again. She finally went for an antacid or two.

"I'm calling, and if she says yes, we're going. If she says no, I'll think of someone else. We need to do this. You go change out those pajamas for some jeans and some shoes and get a light jacket."

"Yes, ma'am." Aurora put the knives and the cutting board in the sink and stuffed the last bit of cheese in her mouth on her way to her bedroom, Chloe close at her heels. She knew if she didn't agree, Sarah would never let it rest. And what if he was the killer? She shivered again.

When Aurora left her bedroom, Sarah stood at the back door, keys in hand. "She said yes. Let's take my car to her house and switch out. You want to put Chloe out or leave her in?"

"I'll put her out." She sighed and took the dog out, patting her on the head. "Glad we have this dog run, Chloe. Never thought we'd use it so much so fast." She closed the gate and jogged back into the house. "Okay."

Within twenty minutes they were in Monica's car, parked on the corner diagonally from Ian's house. The sun had set. They had watched while Ian took down a ladder and put it behind the house. He'd picked up his tools and stored them in his toolbox and taken it behind the house to the detached garage. He appeared to be locking up everything securely, as though he'd be gone for a while. He was out of sight for only a few minutes when he came through the front door, taking the lone rocker on his front porch inside, and coming back out only to lock the front door and head to his truck.

"He's behaving like he's expecting to be gone awhile," Sarah said.

"You know that how?" Aurora followed the truck with her eyes as Ian backed into the street.

"Aww, you already know I drive by here a lot. He never puts his chair inside. He's not going to be back right away, I don't think."

The truck turned the opposite direction from them. Sarah started the car, and they followed.

"His truck is pristine clean," Aurora said.

"Could he have had it washed and detailed because he wanted to hide evidence? Yep," Sarah said.

"Or he could be a person who just every so often has his vehicle washed and detailed, like Jeff, who usually has his truck done every week before he gets home when he's been on the road." She hadn't meant to mention Jeff. She had temporarily put him out of her mind.

"Who knows," they said in unison.

They followed Ian out of town on the interstate toward Austin. The sky grew inky. About half an hour out, it began to thunder, and lightning flashed. A few minutes later, rain poured down. Aurora had to laugh. If it had been Jeff, he'd be really teed-off after he'd had his truck washed. Ian probably felt the same. Most people did. But, considering the weather had been threatening to rain off and on for the last week or so, having one's truck washed did seem curious. They'd had no rain in their neck of the woods for such a long time. Maybe this little storm would move in their direction.

Sarah said, "Wish we had a clue as to where he's going."

"There're a lot of little towns along I-10. He could exit almost any time to go to one of them."

"I'm glad the traffic isn't so bad but just enough so we've have no trouble following. We just need to be patient."

Aurora cut her eyes at Sarah. "You've never been patient."

They lapsed into silence. Aurora's insides shook. The rain had eased a lot after about fifteen minutes but was constant. They were able to keep his taillights in sight. Eventually, he exited. Sarah slowed, so he wouldn't spot them in his rearview mirror. He drove along the feeder road for a few minutes before turning. Now they knew they could be spotted if they turned in too quickly behind him. Sarah pulled to the side of the feeder road and put the emergency flashers on. "Let's count to sixty," she said. "Then go in. I've got butterflies in my chest."

"I'm having a hard time taking a deep breath," Aurora said.

"At least the rain has stopped."

A couple of cars drove around them. One turned in front of them.

Finally, they looked at each other and both let out a gust from their lungs. Sarah turned the flashers off and eased around the corner. They crept along, both keeping an eye out for a white truck. After a row of middle-class homes, they came to a stop sign. They crossed over. The homes on the next block looked a bit more upper end. They continued creeping along. Then Aurora said, "I see it. I see a white truck." She pointed. "Under the streetlight up there."

Sarah stopped the car. "Can you see if anyone is in it?"

"Nope. Let's go."

They grew closer. The home was a nice, two-story. The porch light was on. The front picture window was backlit. Sarah cut the lights and stopped the car parallel to the truck in the street and just a bit in front, so they could see past the truck's grill. What they saw through the window was Ian with a child in his arms and a woman hugging them.

Aurora looked at Sarah. Sarah looked at Aurora. The fading overhead light illuminated the astonishment written across both their faces.

"What the heck!" Aurora said, blinking rapidly to keep her tears at bay.

"You don't suppose that's his sister, do you?" Sarah asked. "Or maybe his brother's wife, and he's come to visit."

Aurora shook her head. "No way. What I suppose is that's his wife and child." Aurora had kind of wanted the killer to be Ian. She would have been so relieved if he had been, but after seeing the three people through the window, she couldn't believe it of him.

While they looked on, he put the child down and laid a whopper of a kiss on the woman.

"Gotta be his wife," Sarah said. "Or his baby mama."

"Nice house," Aurora said. "How could he afford such a place from fixing up and flipping houses?" As she looked on, Ian released the woman and gazed over her head toward the street. He looked right into her eyes. Aurora's hair stood on end. Her heart beat quickened. She jerked back. "Oh my God! I think he saw us—me."

"I don't know how he could with our lights out." Sarah threw the car into drive and pulled way forward. "Let's get out of here before he really does." Once around the corner, she turned on the lights and drove back to the feeder road and the nearest overpass where she could make a U-turn and head back home. Neither of them spoke until they were back on the highway.

Aurora's body returned to normal after the spike of adrenaline, but her hands still shook, and her knees felt like gelatin.

"He's either a phony, or he's leading two lives, like the Boston Strangler," Sarah said. "And the Boston Strangler wasn't the only serial killer who was married and had kids. There was a show on TV about it once. The Green River Killer, The BTK Killer, John Wayne Gacy—"

"Stop! Would you please shut up? I don't want to hear all that stuff."

"I'm just saying what we saw, him and the woman and kid, doesn't mean a thing."

"You mean you still think it could be Ian? Of course you mean Ian." Aurora kind of hoped it was Ian, though she didn't like the idea he knew where she lived and a whole lot about her life. But then, what if it wasn't Ian?

She had hidden her dark thoughts about Jeff from everyone. She'd told herself she was being stupid, paranoid—she had let Sarah get to her—maybe writing mystery novels wasn't such a good idea. Her imagination ran wild, uncontrolled. Jeff's behavior wasn't really suspect, was it? He'd begun gaslighting her almost from the moment they'd married and worse since the loss of the baby. Gaslighting...the term had become so popular it could be misused, but Jeff really had been doing it to her. Did his gaslighting her make him a killer?

Sarah's body had become rigid the more they discussed Ian. She changed lanes and kept her eyes on the road.

"You've got to quit watching serial killer shows." Aurora's stomach had turned inside out. "It's possible Ian does make his living flipping houses. And the woman we just saw, who we can assume is his wife, most likely works also. The two together would be able to afford a nice home. Besides, it's not like he gave us a biography when he started showing up."

"Yeah. I don't know why, but I just assumed he was single. No ring. Unless it's someone else, he could still be the killer. You agree with me, right?"

She couldn't possibly mean Jeff was the someone else. Sarah might be Aurora's best friend, but Aurora had never expressed her thoughts about Jeff to Sarah. She didn't need to. Sarah had never liked Jeff.

"Right, Aurora?"

Aurora shook herself. "What? Sure. But I have a hard time believing it's him after what we just saw."

"Did you note the address?"

Aurora smiled. "Of course. I'm not one hundred percent sure yet he's just a regular person. And you saw me take pictures with my phone even though you were intent on the window."

"I bet Ian Rawlings is not his real name," Sarah said. "We didn't find anything under that name, because it's a fake name. It would make sense if he was a killer moving from place-to-place."

"He's got to have a name to put on the real estate papers. And the tax rolls. We can check both of those on the Internet."

"He could be putting the house in her name, someone else's name, anyway. So, all right, let's check those."

They rode in silence again for a while. Aurora's thoughts swirled around. Maybe she was alone too much. Her mind had been playing tricks on her. Her mother had always said her imagination was often out of control.

"I hope he's not the one. His family looked so nice."

"They did. Like a perfect little family," Aurora said. "If they were his family."

"Had to be. There go my hopes of hooking up with him."

"I didn't think that was ever going to happen, Sarah. If it was, it would have already. We do need to find you someone, though. Hey, let's forget all this serial killer stuff and let the police do their jobs. We can focus on finding you a husband."

Sarah laughed. "Maybe by Christmas? That's only a few months away."

"It could happen," Aurora said. "Maybe Jeff has met some single doctors, or even tech people at the hospitals he calls on. I can ask him." She didn't want to, but she would, if for no other reason than to give her something to talk about when he came home and to get him to focus on something other than what was going on in their own lives.

"I would want someone nearby. At least in Harris County, if not in Houston proper."

"Oh ho, now you're getting picky."

They both laughed. Sarah shrugged. "Sometimes I think it's never going to happen."

"I can still ask."

When they reached Monica's house, they kept mum about what they'd learned. They switched cars and drove back to Aurora's.

"Let's look up the address where he was," Aurora said. "Before you go home. Otherwise, if you're like me, you'll lie in bed and wonder all night."

They traipsed into the house and, after a rest stop and letting Chloe back inside, settled in Aurora's office.

"Glad it didn't rain here," Aurora said, petting the dog. "Even though we need it badly." There was a lean-to for Chloe but not a real shelter in the dog run yet. She opened her laptop and logged on.

Sarah dragged up a chair. They navigated to the tax records. After a few minutes of wading through all the ads and money-making websites, Sarah said, "It's getting late. At this point, I'm too tired to care. And I've got school tomorrow. Can we do this later?"

"I'm tired too. Let me walk you out."

After Sarah left, Aurora searched the address where Ian had gone. There was nothing anywhere. How was that possible? Tired and frustrated, she closed the lid on her laptop.

She had all day Friday to try again and to work on her book. At the present, she needed rest.

As she stripped off her clothes to get ready for bed, her cell dinged. She picked it up and saw, *Change in schedule. I'll be home fairly early tomorrow."*

Keeping his message in mind, Aurora did something she'd been thinking about for a couple of days. She searched Jeff's make-shift dresser, his half of the little closet, and in the black plastic bag where he kept a lot of clothes. Jeff owned a black hoodie. She'd seen him in it in the past. But not lately. She fell into bed with one thing on her mind. If his black hoodie was nowhere to be found, what had happened to it?

CHAPTER
EIGHTEEN

On top of just generally being unable to sleep, letting the adrenaline rush subside, when she finally did succumb, Aurora dreamed of the man in the black hoodie. He ran toward her. He shoved her down on the ground. He kept going. But in her dream, she caught a glimpse of his face. Just a glimpse. And her heart turned flips, waking her up, with Jeff's black hoodie still on her mind.

She'd searched everywhere, but not the suitcase he'd been living out of when they first arrived at Grandpa's house. She was sure she hadn't found the hoodie in her search before she went to bed, because it was stored in his suitcase. Getting up and turning on all the lights, she dropped to her knees and brushed away dust bunnies under the bed. Shoving aside other stuff, she managed to pull the suitcase out. Her heart flipped just like in her dream when she unzipped the suitcase and flung it open. Nada.

What was left? The dirty clothes basket in the bathroom, though she was the one who did the laundry. She'd done the laundry since he'd been gone. The hoodie hadn't been there.

After climbing back into bed, Aurora had one last thought. The hoodie could be in his truck. The weather had gone from an Indian summer to lower temperatures, though not what she thought of as a Texas autumn—cooler and breezy. Jeff had taken his hoodie with him. The hoodie was in his possession. That must be it. Her heart thumped.

Aurora couldn't remember where the hoodie had been when the barn was intruded upon, but at the time she had no reason to suspect Jeff of anything. He'd been grouchy and rude a couple of times. She'd gotten a whiff of what could have been another woman's scent on more than one occasion. Neither of those things alone meant anything. He wouldn't have come home while Aurora was asleep and walked across the street to commit murder. His truck hadn't been in the street when Aurora had gone out to the barn to see who was there. Was it? Her mind was a jumble of wild thoughts. Of course, his truck wouldn't have been parked at their house if he'd committed the murder, though, would it?

Argh, her imagination ran wild. She pulled the covers over her head. She turned over and back and over again. She was determined when he returned tomorrow, she would come up with some excuse to search his truck. The hoodie would be there, lying across the back seat, or crumpled behind the seat. Her writer's brain said if it had been her, she'd have thrown it into a dumpster in another part of town. Jeff was smart enough not to save a hoodie he'd been wearing if he stabbed someone. He was really smart. If the hoodie was in his truck, that would prove he was innocent, and she was just going crazy because of Sarah's imaginings. Problem solved. Or, it would be after she searched.

Part of her wanted to open the computer back up and continue the search of Jeff she'd started a few days earlier and hadn't finished. Another part said to go to sleep. She'd be no good the next day, especially if Jeff was in one of his black moods. But, as soon as she arose the following morning, she would google the name of the woman he'd said he was married to and find out what happened to her. She didn't know how early Jeff would return home, but she could finish her search and be hard at work on her book or walking the dog or clearing out the barn or *something* when he showed up. She shivered and laid awake for what felt like all night.

Weary in her bones, at daylight Aurora dragged herself out of bed, Chloe right at her heels, little doggie moans making it apparent Chloe wanted to go outside. The morning was clear and cool. Aurora took care of Chloe before going to her office. Opening the computer's home screen, seeing the photo of herself and her husband on their wedding day, remembering how happy she'd been that someone so charming had taken to her, Aurora's doubts receded from her foggy brain. She stared at their faces for a few moments, rubbing her arms to get warm. She wore a sleeveless nightgown. She hadn't pulled on a robe in her haste to get back to the computer, to prove her husband was innocent. Or guilty. What was wrong with her that she'd become so paranoid?

After a deep breath, Aurora scrounged in the side drawer and took out the paper on which she'd written the name of the woman who had been Jeff's common law wife. Why she'd made a note of it and hidden it under pens and notepads, she didn't want to even think about. Just natural woman's curiosity. Right. She plugged the name into the search engine.

Nothing came up on the first page. On the second page, however, an obituary popped up. Blinking hard to clear her tired, burning eyes, Aurora hauled herself into the kitchen. She needed caffeine in the worst way and started the coffee. Tea just wouldn't hold enough charge. Back at her desk, she leaned in to read the short paragraph. Jeff's common law wife had been killed in Spring, Texas, which was a little over an hour and a half north, by a hit-and-run driver.

A sour taste in her mouth, Aurora dug deeper and found a report. The only witness reported a white truck receding down the road. No other description and no license number. No verification a white truck or any truck had been involved.

Slamming the lid on her laptop, Aurora gazed into space, in a state of shock, trying not to believe she could be married to a man who killed women. After a few minutes, the coffee aroma drew her into the kitchen where she poured herself a cup and just about collapsed at the table, laying her head in her folded arms. A pure coincidence? Millions of white trucks in Texas. Probably hundreds of thousands in Harris County alone. Still ...

What felt like a few hours later, Aurora stumbled to the back door in response to Chloe's scratching and barking. She threw her arms around the dog and hugged her, seeking comfort in the only place available. Chloe smelled strongly of dog and appeared to have rolled around in the grass.

"Without asking why, Georgina," Aurora said to her friend's voice mail, "please do what you can to find the approximate dates the women we've been talking about were killed. As well, the locations." After a moment of thought, Aurora included, "ASAP, please and let me know ASAP. A list in a text or email would be good."

In the shower, she shampooed her hair and soaped her body, in hopes she'd emerge wider awake and cleansed of her suspicions. No success. Tears of distrust ran down her face. If Georgina could provide the requested information, Aurora could compare the list with what she knew of Jeff's trips. She didn't know where he went most of the time, but she knew when he left and when he returned. And she could check "recents" on her phone log to see where he was when he called.

After showering, Aurora immediately picked up her cell, looking for a message from Georgina. In a brief one, Georgina said, *I suspect I know why you're asking for this information. When I have it, I'll call you back. Should be by lunch time.*

Checking "recents," Aurora found if the person who was calling was in her contacts, the phone didn't show where they were calling from, just the date. At that moment, she couldn't think how knowing the day would be helpful. Bummer.

She dressed and took Chloe for a walk up the slope to Main Street and back down a block to a street running parallel to the one running past their house. She'd hoped to clear her head while she addressed Chloe's discipline issues. All other thoughts went away, but only for a minute or two.

She was being stupid, letting Sarah get to her. She wouldn't have been so blind as to have married a man who was a sociopath, or a psychopath, or just plain mean and evil. He'd been so sweet in the beginning, so charming, so helpful. He had wanted the baby. He really did. He'd said a child would complete him, complete our family, add another reason to come home from being on the road each week.

Aurora's phone didn't ring during the whole walk. Sarah was teaching. Her other friends were working or, she guessed, living their lives. Jeff was in his truck on the way home.

As lunch time grew closer, Aurora became more anxious. She wanted the information before Jeff returned, but she couldn't hold Georgina to a specific time. What reason would she give to look in his truck if she couldn't access it without his knowledge. The hoodie being there, or not, would not really be conclusive of anything. What was she going to do if the information Georgina gave her confirmed her suspicions? But then, what if it didn't?

Aurora paced. She checked for messages. She swept. Dusted. Brushed her hair. Her stomach growled, but she didn't think she could hold anything down. Finally, Georgina texted her with a list. *As much info as I can find right now.*

Aurora squeezed her eyes shut while she waited the few seconds for her printer to print the list, hoping when she opened and looked there would be no evidence her husband might be guilty of the atrocious acts that had been haunting the metropolitan area for several years.

After putting Chloe in the dog run, Aurora took the list and her phone and a lap rug and went outside to the front porch. The metallic smell in the air and dark clouds on the horizon indicated a rainstorm approached, finally. Maybe this one would not pass them by like all the others. Taking a deep breath, she scanned the list and, realizing Georgina had included incidents from before

Aurora even knew Jeff, went back to the top and started crossing those off.

She felt like a fool. She really hadn't known Jeff long. They'd met and married quickly. At the time, she'd had few qualms. After all, she'd been pregnant. He'd charmed her right off her feet, to paraphrase a cliché. From the time he'd—she hated to admit—picked her up in the mall, until the present, it had only been, what, six months? Had she been so blinded by grief over her cheating husband and the betrayal by her best friend she was easy pickings for a predator, or was she letting her imagination get out of control?

The first incident occurred—she looked in her phone back to the day she met Jeff—shortly after they'd met. A woman's body had been discovered on the side of Loop 610, which circled Houston. Of course, Aurora had no way of knowing what Jeff's schedule had been back then. She knew he was in some kind of sales, and he traveled.

The trauma of her divorce caused her to focus on herself in the days and weeks after they'd met, and the relationship developed. Jeff had been there for her. Holding her when she'd been crying. Getting angry after court when she'd ended up with less than she deserved. Helping her pick up the few things her ex had been ordered to restore to her.

She hadn't really thought about Jeff's schedule then, or how he came to be off. She still didn't know. Ian had made her aware of how little she knew of Jeff's routine. He probably made his own schedule. Isn't that what responsible salespeople did?

The second victim on the list had been found in the month after she and Jeff had gotten together. The victim had been found along a farm-to-market road between Houston and Galveston. She scrolled through her "recents." Jeff had called her several times in the weeks after they'd met, and he'd been out of town, but she couldn't tell where he was calling from. She could only see the call had been from him.

What she was doing was probably a waste of time since there was no way of telling where he was calling from, but she couldn't seem to stop. The more she looked, the more her stomach twisted and tightened.

Thunder rumbled in the distance. The sweet smell of ozone grew stronger. Breathing became more difficult, which could have been from the ozone, but which definitely came from the panic setting in, the longer she reviewed the list.

Aurora went inside to her computer and brought up her calendar. She pinpointed the first time she and Jeff had slept together, glad no one was around to see her face grow red when she realized how soon it had been after they'd met. And how quickly she'd taken him to meet her grandfather, who he'd also charmed. And Howard, her brother. And then she'd found she was pregnant. She'd marked that on her calendar. He'd been out of town, and the authorities had discovered another body. She remembered the phone call and how, after a brief hesitation, he'd sounded excited at the prospect of being a father.

When the thunder resounded even closer, Aurora remembered she'd put Chloe in the dog run. Guilt-ridden, she opened the door and found the dog pressed up against the fence and whimpering. Crouching down, she hugged the agitated dog in an effort to calm both of them. She'd meant to buy a thunder jacket for Chloe but hadn't gotten around to it. After peeling open a small packet of a dog snack and dropping the contents into Chloe's inside bowl, Aurora went back to her computer.

She knew she should shut down the computer since lightning could hit nearby and cause a power surge. What would she do then if it messed up her computer and she hadn't backed up everything. She quickly ran through the list Georgina had given her. She would have had indigestion if she'd eaten anything. As it was, she felt a spasm in her chest and shut down the computer.

Aurora sat back, thinking of how fast the past months had gone by and the events had taken place. They'd met at a mall. They'd gotten married when she'd turned up pregnant. Her grandfather had died and left her and Howard the property. Howard agreed not to put the house on the market to sell if Aurora would buy him out. Jeff agreed to come up with part of the purchase price. After the deal, Jeff suggested they move and redo the house and live there. Then she'd lost the baby.

She'd met him at a mall. Women had been kidnapped from malls. The cops thought the killer had moved his territory. She and Jeff had moved to the county's outer limits.

Jeff had been pressing her to put the house in both names. He wanted wills that left everything to each other. They needed to get life insurance on her, he'd said. Of course, with himself as the beneficiary.

Remembering felt like a heavy blanket thrown over her. She put her head between her knees and breathed deeply. Chloe stuck her head under Aurora's folded arms and nosed her, making a little squeaking noise. Stroking Chloe's back helped calm Aurora, helped Chloe stop prancing with nervousness at the upcoming storm, but didn't do anything to stop Aurora from recognizing she could be married to a serial killer. Or at least someone who had plans for her.

CHAPTER
NINETEEN

Tires crunched on the gravel. A car door slammed. Aurora stood in the kitchen and tried to steady her hands. Her stomach did its annoying, painful churning. She hadn't quite made up her mind what she was going to do, whether or not she should confront Jeff. Chloe scurried into the kitchen and sat right behind her. Peeking through the back window, she could see Jeff walking toward the back door from his sparkling, clean white pickup.

When he entered the house and approached her as though to kiss her as he often did, Aurora's body involuntarily stiffened. She stopped herself, before she stepped back, and turned her cheek, his lips barely grazing her. If she hadn't stood still, he would have sensed something wasn't right. He may have anyway.

"You okay?" He stood so close she had to back up to see his face. His bristle was heavier than normal. His musky odor was stronger than usual, like he hadn't showered. Maybe she just imagined it.

Though they'd known each other less than a year and had only been married a few months, Aurora thought she knew him well enough to know from his tone of voice when he wasn't being genuine. He didn't sound like he cared whether she was okay. His expression didn't look as if he were truly interested in her welfare. Or was she imagining both because she had convinced herself he wasn't the man she'd thought she'd married. "Yes, sure. I guess I was daydreaming. I came into the kitchen to decide what to cook and found myself just standing here."

Instead of going to put his briefcase away as he usually did, Jeff set it on the table in their little dining room and returned to the kitchen. "What's on your mind?" He stood with his hands on his hips. Not exactly menacing but close enough.

Aurora stepped over to the refrigerator, opening it and sticking her head inside. "You see anything in here you'd like me to fix?" Her insides shivered at the idea of his seeing the list and questioning her.

He took her arm, pulling her out of the refrigerator, forcing her to face him.

Chloe growled.

"What's your problem?" he said, with a glare at the dog. Chloe returned to standing behind Aurora.

"I haven't taken her for a walk yet," Aurora said. He would have no way of knowing she lied. She let the refrigerator door close and wrenched her arm free.

"Did I do something I need to apologize for? You seem lately to have an attitude about you."

"Okay, if you must know. I did a search of the Harris County marriage records. I couldn't find anything showing you'd been married before."

"Well, that's easy to answer, Aurora." He leaned against the counter, his hands in his pockets.

"I didn't see any divorce records either."

"I don't know what's up with you, but if you want to know something you should just ask me."

"You said you'd been married before."

180

"Honey," he started to take her arm again, but this time she did step back. "What is the matter with you?"

"You lied to me." The inside of her mouth tasted bitter.

"I didn't lie. I told you we were married by common law. God. Everybody knows you can be married by common law in Texas."

She knew that, she just wanted to see what he'd say. His response didn't make her feel any better. "Y'all never registered it." She was past believing him or in him. She wanted to get as far away from him as the kitchen would allow, to get something to drink, to get the taste of fear out of her mouth. She filled a small glass with water from the faucet and took a swallow. It didn't taste any better than her mouth did. "What about your divorce? Did you ever get a divorce? Is there anything in Texas that's a common law divorce?" She knew better, but again, wanted to hear what he'd say.

He grabbed a can of beer out of the refrigerator and opened it as he crossed into the little dining room and sat down. "Let's talk about this. I don't know what you're so upset about, but I don't want you to be mad at me." He pushed out a chair with his foot. "Sit down."

"I don't want to sit down." With her arms crossed, she stood in the doorway, not moving, the back door behind her. Chloe stayed next to her.

He remained seated, staring up at her, his brows drawn together. "What's this all about?"

"There wasn't anything in the divorce records." What would he say to that?

He shook his head. His eyes stared into the distance as if he were in a trance. "She died, Aurora."

So, he was admitting it. The hair on Aurora's neck stood at attention. She started to say *I'm sorry for your loss*, like she automatically would to anyone else who told her someone who had been close to them had died, then everything she'd learned flashed through her mind. She couldn't let on she knew everything, or anything at all. Her eyes fixed on his, while her brain calculated what she should be doing to protect herself. She stood and stared and waited to hear what else he'd say.

He took a swig from his can of beer. "I guess now you want to know how she died."

"Of course." She dug her hands into her back pockets, so he wouldn't see them tremble.

"Car accident."

"Uh-huh." If he told her the body was found on the side of the road, she was going to make a run for it.

"Hit and run."

"Where?"

"You can look it up. It was Houston. You want me to give you her full name and age and where we were living at the time? I will. I don't know what's gotten into you. You act like you're afraid of me."

Hadn't the article said she'd died in Spring, Texas? A crack in his story. "I heard the police said the truck that hit the last woman whose body was found on the side of the road was white."

Something flickered across his face. "What?" He jumped up, causing his chair to tip over. "You're implying because a white truck hit a woman who was found on the side of the road you think I did it?" He stepped toward her.

Aurora stepped back. Chloe whimpered.

"Did Sarah say that? Has she been trying to turn you against me? I know she doesn't like me. Or was it one of your other girlfriends? What the hell, Aurora?" His eyes wavered as he looked at her with what she took to be a contrived hurt expression.

She held her ground, but her hackles rose. "Let me ask you this." She tried to keep the tremor out of her voice. "Where's your black hoodie?" Her eyes were wide as she looked up at him.

His eyes penetrated hers. After what felt like minutes, he took another step toward her and said, "Why are you interested in my black hoodie?" He moved closer. "It's in my truck."

Aurora took a giant step back. She was running out of space to back away. "Why don't you go get it for me, so I can take a look at it?"

She wasn't sure what she felt. After all she'd learned, she was convinced he was the serial killer. But maybe he wasn't. Should she tell him what she knew? The women had been killed while he was out of town. The police said most of the women had been taken from malls. He and she had met in a mall. Was she targeted to be a victim when for some reason he took a liking to her? Had she mentioned her elderly grandfather in that first conversation they'd had at the bookstore? Had he hoped she'd come into money?

"I can't believe you suspect me of being a killer, Aurora. God. I thought you getting a dog would make you feel better about being here alone when I'm gone—you wouldn't be so rattled. Apparently, *she*" he pointed his finger at Chloe, "didn't help." He threw himself back into the chair, his legs splayed and took another swig of his beer. "How can you think such a thing when we've been so close, when I've been so good to you?"

Good to her? His black moods. His refusal to leave her alone when he wanted to have sex. In fact, the rough sex. The gaslighting. Obsessive thoughts swirled in her head.

He didn't go get the hoodie. Aurora sensed his demeanor was changing, not an extreme like Dr. Jekyll and Mr. Hyde, but something ... Oh, hell, could it just be her writer's imagination?

"I want you to talk to someone," Jeff said.

"Talk to someone? What do you mean?" She'd done some reading and now knew that's what gaslighters did, made you think you were losing your mind.

"Have I ever done anything to make you think I would hurt you? Or hurt anyone? I don't know where all this is coming from. Maybe a talk with a counselor of some kind would be good for you."

Well, so long as he didn't think forcing sex and rough sex hurt her. But could he be right? She didn't think so. It was gaslighting. Gaslighting. Gaslighting.

Chloe barked twice. Both of them turned their eyes on her. "Chloe's signaling, she needs to go out."

"You want to put her in the dog run?"

"I haven't walked her today. I'll take her briefly since the sky is growing dark. Think we might finally get some rain?"

"Are you just going to walk her so we can't continue this conversation?"

"I'm sorry, Jeff. I'm so confused." Chloe stood at the door, her nails tapping on the tile. "Let me get her leash. I'll take her for a walk before it starts raining. I need a few minutes to think, anyway." Aurora strode out of the room, leaving him sitting there.

She stopped in the bathroom to take care of business before leaving. When she returned to the kitchen, leash in hand, Chloe was gone. The door stood open. Jeff eyeballed Aurora, a smug look on his face, and tilted the beer can up so he could get another swallow.

"Where's Chloe?"

He tucked his chin into his shoulder, an odd glint in his eyes, and smirked. "She wanted out so badly, I accommodated her."

"What? I told you how she lost her toes. You know she'll run into the street. She'll chase the first car that comes by." Aurora ran out the door to see if she could find the dog before it was too late, before she got hit by a car. "Chloe!" She didn't see her anywhere. "Chloe!"

"Aww, too bad, she's nowhere around." Jeff leaned against the porch doorjamb with his arms crossed.

"Jeff! What the heck?" She shot a look of anger at him, but it was nothing compared to his jeer.

"She probably already spotted a car to chase." His grin reminded her of an evil clown.

Aurora glanced up and down the street again. Jeff's cruelty confirmed her worst fears. She didn't know how she could prove who he really was and what he'd done, but at that moment she was most concerned about Chloe. She said no more. She pushed past him to grab her keys. She was going to search for Chloe. Once she found her, she'd have to decide what to do about living with a man she assumed was a serial killer, but right now was not the time.

She turned to leave with her keys, and Jeff grabbed her forearm. "Where are you going, *sweetheart*?"

Aurora didn't like what she saw in his eyes. She jerked her arm away. "I'm going after Chloe. We can talk more when I return." She ran down the steps to her car. As she backed out, Jeff, sneering, stood on the porch, still leaning on the doorjamb like an adolescent hood outside a local hangout. She gunned her Prius as she left the driveway.

CHAPTER
TWENTY

The smell of rain permeated the air. Thunder rumbled closer than Aurora would have liked. Glancing both ways and not seeing Chloe anywhere as the car slowly rolled up the slope toward Main Street, Aurora arrived at the four-lane state highway running through town just after a lightning strike and the sky burst open. Sheets of rain pounded on the car's roof and blew onto her windshield making seeing difficult. The native grasses lining the roadway bent from the force. Traffic wasn't as light as she would have thought in such conditions. Heedless of the weather, vehicles raced both ways as though there was an emergency somewhere.

Chloe couldn't have gotten far. Heedless of the rain, Aurora put the driver's side window down and the passenger's side window partly down, so she could see out. She creeped along below the posted speed limit, ignoring the blasting horns. If she saw her dog, she could quickly pull over and grab her. Anyone who wanted to go faster would have to pass. After a few minutes, a white pickup appeared behind her but kept its distance. Was the driver Jeff, or someone else in one of the world's ubiquitous white trucks?

She had no real doubt the occupant was Jeff. Jeff knew she was onto him. He must have realized she wouldn't be returning home. He would want to stop her. Cruelly, he'd opened the door for Chloe on purpose, knowing the dog had a propensity to chase cars. Aurora had clearly told him that, when she first talked to him about Chloe on the phone.

She brushed her hair from her face. Tears burned behind her eyes. Even with the car heater going, she shivered and not from the chill air blowing inside the car. She was too far ahead to see for sure that Jeff was the truck's driver. Through the rain and the truck's headlights, she could see nothing but the silhouette of a person. She slowed down. The truck slowed down. She speeded up. The truck did, too.

Ahead, an object, a big lump of something in the pouring rain laid in the middle of the road, on the painted lines. As Aurora drew nearer, the lump looked like Chloe, caught, unable to cross two lanes in either direction to get to safety. Aurora couldn't let the dog remain out there to be hit, run over, by a car.

She slowed down. The truck behind her slowed also. She pulled to the side of the road on the shoulder and parked even further off the road, in the weeds. The white truck eased to the side of the road but still too far back for her to see who it was. Gooseflesh rose on her arms and neck. The sour taste was back in her mouth. Whoever was in the truck—and in her heart she knew it was Jeff—meant her harm. However, she had a choice to make. She could rescue the dog and bring her to safety, or accelerate away, fleeing from whatever harm Jeff had in mind for her. She had only a moment to decide.

She stuck her head out the window, brushing the rain off her face and out of her eyes. For sure, the lump was Chloe. If Aurora didn't hurry, Chloe might run to her. She'd be hit and killed. The dog stood, stared at her, dark eyes holding a plea, her tail almost hidden between her legs. Rainwater dripped down her body. She was soaked clean through, fur matted. Her body vibrated with shivers.

The cars and trucks continued to race by, but Aurora couldn't leave Chloe. She had to save her. She didn't have anything in the car to dry her with, but they could go to the shelter where they'd both be safe. The shelter had plenty of dry towels. And what was she even thinking that for when what she needed to do first was get Chloe out of harm's way.

For a moment, she forgot the truck had pulled off the road behind her. Then she remembered Jeff. Still, she couldn't leave the dog. She put her window up and turned her engine off. Then her lights. The white truck didn't cut its lights. In the mist and falling rain, she still couldn't see for sure who was back there, but it had to be Jeff. Shrugging, Aurora made her move.

Heart pumping, she cracked open the driver's door and looked both ways down the two lanes on her side of the state highway. Several vehicles flew past. It would only take her a few moments to dash to the center of the highway, grab the dog, and cross back. She could race into the grasses at the side of the road and then put Chloe in the car on the passenger side.

After the next vehicle, Chloe's and Aurora's eyes met. She flung her car door all the way open, held up her hand like a stop sign, hoping the dog wouldn't run to her, slammed the door behind her, glanced both ways again, and rushed to the center of the highway, rain cascading down on her head and into her mouth as she shouted, "Stay! Stay!"

Crouching down, she spoke in soothing tones and wrapped her arms around the soaked, shivering dog. She didn't want her to be even more scared than she was, standing in the middle of the road.

Aurora patted her and a noise of another vehicle's door slamming came from behind. Being soaked, Chloe was heavier than normal. Aurora turned. Jeff stood outside his truck, his face creased with what Aurora would have taken as concern in the past. She might have thought he was going to help. He could carry the dog more easily than she could. She might have felt relief, but in her heart, she knew better. Something in his eyes, the gleam, telegraphed Jeff wasn't there to help. She glanced down the road. Her husband meant to do her harm as he was sure to have done to those other women whose bodies were found in roadways. How easy would it be for him to push her and Chloe into oncoming traffic?

She had to pretend she didn't know. He might still have doubts. Her eyes flickered toward the oncoming traffic on their side, and she beckoned to her husband and shouted, "Jeff, thank God you're here! Chloe is so heavy! I can use your help!" She beckoned to him again.

Arms extended in front of him, Jeff jogged toward them, the look in his eyes not wavering, the expression on his face confirming Aurora's worst fears. Her face broke out into a broad smile as though to welcome his help. He crossed the first lane, then as he entered the second one, his arms still stretched out toward her, one of the largest SUVs on the market skidded into him. Jeff's body soared into the air as the vehicle spun, crossed the other lanes, crossed back, and stopped just short of where Aurora and Chloe were still planted on the stripe.

Horns honked as cars and trucks on both sides of the highway braked and skidded, some hydroplaning. Lights flashed. Tires screeched.

Jeff's body landed in the long grasses on the side of the road.

Aurora grabbed Chloe and ran to her car. She shoved the dog inside and strode toward her husband, lying on his back. His eyes met hers. With raised eyebrows, she cocked her head, a hint of a smile on her lips. "Bye, bye." The light left his eyes, and his lids closed over them.

Her eyes met the SUV driver's wide, stricken eyes. Shivering, rain cascading off his Stetson, he was moments behind her as he hurried over, kneeled, and checked the pulse on Jeff's neck. Traffic had backed up on both sides. The driver looked up at Aurora. "You call 911?"

"I haven't had time yet," she said. "Didn't you?"

He skirted around Jeff's body and jogged to the passenger side of his SUV, digging out his cell from inside. While he made the call, Aurora stood fixed to the ground. She stared at Jeff and heaved a long sigh.

After a few minutes, Aurora walked back to her Prius and crawled inside. She kept a box of tissues on the passenger seat. She took the box and crawled with it into the back, wiping Chloe's mournful eyes and face, drying her head as best she could, running the shreds of tissues across the dog's body. Releasing her, Aurora crawled back into the front seat and started the car, turning the heater to the max.

She couldn't leave. The police would want to speak to her. At least she and Chloe would get as warm and dry as they could with the heater on. Maybe when the ambulance came, the techs would give her a blanket or two blankets, one for her and one for Chloe, so they could get more comfortable until the police came. Or if the police came first, maybe they would give her some blankets for the two of them. If police carried blankets. Maybe in their trunks. Aurora shivered and shook her head. Her thinking was screwy. Maybe she was going into shock. She rubbed her arms. She'd used the whole box of tissues on Chloe, leaving nothing with which to even attempt to dry herself.

A short while later, someone drew Aurora's attention from the fugue she realized she was in. A police officer, his uniform covered with a slicker, a covered hat on his head, knocked and motioned with a finger for Aurora to put the window down.

"Are you all right, ma'am?" His brow wrinkled with concern. His coffee breath filled the air in the small car.

Aurora nodded and shivered. "We—we got wet."

His eyes widened. "Yes. Let me see if the EMTs have something to dry you off with."

"And for Chloe?"

He glanced in the back seat. "Your dog? Yes, her, too." His eyes reverted to Aurora's face for a moment before he jogged to the ambulance standing in the middle of the street.

Aurora looked around. Another officer stood in the road and directed traffic. Cars and trucks lined the road ahead and behind. Jeff's truck still had the lights on. They reflected in her rear-view mirror. She reached back and stroked Chloe again. The dog had put her head between the seats and rested it on the center console, her plaintive eyes peering up at Aurora as if to ask if she were okay.

Not long later, Georgina arrived at the car's window, and said, "Let me in the other door." She wore her police uniform, also covered by a slicker.

Aurora didn't realize she'd locked the car. She unlocked it.

Georgina climbed in, reaching over and giving Aurora a big hug. "Honey, I'm so sorry! You must be so traumatized!"

An EMT came to the window with two blankets, and Aurora put the window down and accepted them with a nod of thanks. She unfolded one and draped it around Chloe, then herself.

"I'm all right." She shivered again. "Just need to get warm and dry. I want to go back home."

"Can you tell me what happened?"

Aurora looked at Georgina, her friend, and knew she could trust her, but Georgina was a police officer. Aurora would have to measure her words. Her eyes welled up, and she swallowed the softball-sized lump in her throat. "Chloe got out. A car drove by. Chloe chased the car up the hill."

Georgina kept her eyes on Aurora's face and didn't say anything.

"I had to find her. She would get wet and sick if I didn't find her."

Georgina nodded. "Go on."

"I drove up here and saw her in the middle of the street. She looked like a huge wet mop. She was scared to death, violently shaking, so I parked and went to get her. Cars were racing by. I knew it was dangerous, but I couldn't let a car hit her."

"Jeff must have followed you."

"I was trying to pick up Chloe. She was so heavy, being soaked and all. When I saw Jeff must have followed me and had stopped, I yelled to him. I needed help. He ran into the street—I guess to help us—and a big SUV hit him." She pointed at the vehicle where another officer was talking to the driver. "He wasn't at fault. Jeff just darted out into the road without looking."

"I see. You must have grabbed Chloe and brought her back here."

Georgina's eyes roved over Aurora's face and down to Chloe's head, still resting on the console. Georgina scratched Chloe behind the ears. She glanced toward where Jeff's body lay.

"I put Chloe in here and ran to Jeff. I don't know if he could see me. His eyes were still open but then closed. I knew he must have died. The man who hit him checked for a pulse." She blinked several times to hold back the tears. "He—he's the one who called 911." She wiped her eyes with her fingers and heaved another big sigh.

Georgina examined Aurora's face again before glancing back at the accident scene. "We're going to need you to make a statement."

"I've told you everything."

Georgina's eyes were wide and round as they flickered from one side of Aurora's face to the other. "Still, we'll need one."

"O—okay. In here or?"

"You need a change of clothes. I don't think you should be driving, at least for the rest of the afternoon. Since you live just a few blocks from here, I'll drive you there in your car. You can have a few minutes to dry off and change, then someone will come get us, and we'll go to the station."

"Whatever you say, Georgina. I'm sure you know what's best in this kind of situation." She squeezed Georgina's hand. "Thank you."

Georgina looked her over again. "We take care of our friends, but, anyway, that's nothing we wouldn't do for anyone in the same situation." She climbed out of the car and went to speak to another officer who stood near Jeff's body.

Chloe, whose head still rested on the console between the seats, peered up at Aurora with doleful eyes. Aurora leaned down and put her face in the mop of Chloe's wet head and wept.

EPILOGUE

Most everyone had left the funeral home after Jeff's memorial service, but Aurora continued to be pasted on the front row with Sarah beside her, holding her hand. In their near-matching black dresses and black pumps, the two women could almost have been twins except for one of them being below average in height and the other above. Aurora's wispy auburn hair, with the dark brown roots growing out, and her hazel eyes contrasted with Sarah's pale blue eyes and light brown hair. They'd been inseparable in the past few days and would be most likely for the next few.

Jeff's body had been cremated, and, although he hadn't known many people in town, Aurora's friends thought it appropriate to have some kind of service. Since Aurora and Jeff weren't church-goers, a funeral home had to serve. Georgina, who apparently had experience with such things, rounded up their mutual friends and arranged everything. Aurora would be relieved when everything was over, and the chain of events began fading from her mind.

Almost a week had passed since Jeff's death. She'd experienced sleepless nights filled with nightmares, periods of tears, days of total exhaustion, and of finding herself wrapped in a lap rug and sitting in a daze on the front porch after the cold front blew in. Chloe never left Aurora's side. The daze, the haziness persisted.

"We need to go," Sarah said. "People will be at my house, waiting on us to arrive and allow them to give you their condolences and eat all those casseroles they're sure to have brought." She squeezed Aurora's hand. When she failed to get a response, Sarah tugged it, trying to get Aurora to listen. "Aurora, everyone's gone except you and me. We need to go."

"Not everyone." A deep voice came from above and behind them. Ian put his hand on the back of the bench seat and leaned down next to Aurora. "I'm sorry for your loss, Aurora. Hello, Sarah." He wore a navy-blue blazer over a white shirt with a striped tie and navy pants. His clothing looked very official, somehow, but served as respectful funeral wear.

Aurora turned her head toward him. "Thank you, Ian."

Sarah nodded at Ian and squeezed Aurora's hand again. They hadn't seen him since the night they'd followed him out of town. Everything had happened so fast since then.

He touched Aurora's shoulder. "We need to talk." He looked at Sarah. "You need to be present. I want to speak with both of you before I leave town." His breath had a fresh, minty smell.

Sarah exchanged a glance with Aurora. They'd been right about his preparing to leave, and now he was on the verge of going.

"What's going on?" Sarah asked. She scooted to the edge of her seat, still holding Aurora's hand. "What do you need from us?"

"Listen, I'm sorry I haven't been to see you before now. I had business elsewhere. Let's clear out of here and get some coffee. There's that place on Main."

"I—I'm not sure what you might want to talk to me about, but I'll help in any way I can," Aurora said, slowly getting to her feet. "I'm very familiar with that area. That SUV hit Jeff right out in the street near the coffee shop."

"That's what I understand." He wore a solemn expression. "I need to inform the two of you of a few things."

"What do you want to talk about that you can't say right here?" Sarah asked, easing a little in front of Aurora in what could be construed as a protective stance.

"I think you know." He raised his right eyebrow. "This isn't the greatest time to speak with the two of you, but it's the best I can do. We won't be long."

Sarah tugged on Aurora's arm. "Come on. Let's go to the coffee shop. I, for one, could use a stiff drink, but strong coffee will have to do."

Aurora nodded. No matter what Ian wanted, nothing could be worse than when she realized she'd slept with, and been impregnated by, a serial killer. She'd thought and thought about it ever since the *accident*. She was positive Jeff was the killer. Ian most likely wanted to confirm it.

"I can drive you ladies, or you can meet me there."

"We'll meet you," Sarah said. "We're in my car." She guided Aurora up the aisle, Ian behind them.

Once they were on their way to the coffee shop, Sarah said, "I wasn't about to get into a car with him no matter what we saw last week when we followed him. I don't know if we'd be safe."

When Aurora failed to respond, Sarah said, "Do you still think he's the serial killer? I'm not sure."

Aurora had not confided in Sarah, or anyone else. She suspected Georgina had a lot of questions, but Aurora had holed up in her house and hadn't allowed anyone to spend any more time with her other than to give their condolences and drop off food and/or drink as was the custom when someone in one's family had died, except for Sarah. After peppering her with questions about the entire event, Sarah came regularly with food and drink and generally attended to Aurora's needs like she was an invalid. Emotionally, Aurora was pushing through as best she could, which wasn't much.

Everything was so complicated. She didn't know if she'd be able to explain about Jeff sufficiently. She wanted to put it all behind her. Forget about him. She had an appointment with the lawyer in the upcoming week. Harold, her brother, came briefly and told her he'd take care of anything she needed if she wanted him to. He'd return to go to the lawyer's office with her. Aurora just wanted to be rid of every bit of Jeff and his stuff she could, even though she knew her head would swirl with thoughts about him for months to come.

"Aurora, did you hear me? Did we give up on the idea that Ian is the serial killer?"

"What?" Aurora shook herself. "Yeah. I did, anyway. You didn't?"

"I'm just not sure." Sarah said again and looked at Aurora sideways. After several minutes, she pulled the car into a spot a few doors down from the shop. "Come on, let's go. I know all this is difficult for you, but it'll be over soon, and you'll be able to move on with your life."

Aurora nodded. "You're right." She didn't add, *I hope.* Ian had walked down and held the passenger door open. Aurora slid out and looked up at him, curiosity beginning to take hold. What he had to say might help her make sense of things, or not.

Once she and Sarah had their coffee and were seated at a table in the back, away from the window over-looking the street, Ian joined them. They sat on one side. He faced them from the other.

"I think I can speak for both of us, Ian, when I ask just what is this about? Aurora hasn't been herself since the accident, so even if you hadn't asked that I be here, I would have insisted. You already know we're best friends." Sarah picked up her coffee cup and slurped, her eyes never leaving his face.

Aurora sat quietly, picking at her nails, her eyes shifting from one person to the other. She wasn't entirely herself. Not sure there was any reason she needed protection, she was still glad Sarah was with her.

Ian sipped his coffee and leaned his forearms on the table, about the closest he could get to them. "First, let me just say, I know you ladies followed me out of town last week."

Sarah's hand flew under the table and clutched Aurora's thigh.

Aurora's skin tingled with electricity. She remembered looking into that plate glass window and feeling that Ian could see her, was looking directly into her eyes. She swallowed. "I don't know how you could have seen us once we stopped outside that house, but I know you did. I felt it when you looked out the window at me."

"Sarah, you're not as good at tailing someone as you may think you are. Or, I could use the term *stalking*."

Sarah started to protest, but Ian held up his hand. "No worries. Not a big deal. But I suggest you stick with being a teacher, not a cop." He sipped his coffee again, a smile in his eyes.

"You know I'm a teacher?"

Ian laughed. "I know all about both of you and your closest friends." He pulled a smallish, black ID holder out of his pocket and flipped it open.

"FBI?" Aurora giggled. "I'm sorry. I suddenly feel giddy. And silly." The haze she'd been feeling began to lift. "No wonder we couldn't find anything about you on the Internet."

"Not for lack of trying, I suspect," Ian said.

"Not for lack of trying by both of us," Aurora said. She glanced at Sarah. "Close your mouth, Sarah."

"Okay," Ian said. "I know you need to get to Sarah's house, both of you, so let me fill you in on a few things. This is not for public consumption. You good with that?"

"Ever?" Sarah asked, looking wide-eyed. She had shifted back on the bench seat and held her cardboard coffee cup with both hands.

He nodded. "Someday, if you're still interested when this case is concluded, I'll be able to fill you in more. By then, it'll be in the public domain, anyway."

Aurora's hands trembled. She pulled them down into her lap. She'd known Ian wasn't the serial killer. He couldn't possibly be since Jeff was. But Sarah was still in the dark. She slid her hand across to Sarah's kneecap under the table and held on like it was some kind of knob. She expelled a deep breath, ready for Ian's big reveal.

"Ever since you made that *joke*, Sarah, which you probably could tell I didn't find particularly funny, I've wanted to clue you in. Of course, I couldn't. We'd been on the trail of the man who had been terrorizing Harris County."

Sarah drank from her cardboard cup of coffee but peered over the cup's edge at Ian as he spoke. Gooseflesh attacked Aurora's arms and the back of her neck. She wished Ian would just get on with it. Was he going to confront her, ask her what she knew and when she knew it?

"Recently, the man had altered his territory to this part of Harris County. We figured he had been scouting this area for a while and then physically moved. He may have felt we were closing in on him. Any reference to the serial killings, even as jokes, was not open to discussion. If he didn't know we were getting close, we didn't want any gossip out there to indicate we might be focusing on him. This area is like a small town with very few secrets."

"When did you figure out for sure who it was you were after?" Aurora asked. Her mouth had gone dry, but her eyes had begun to tear up and burned. She stared down at the tabletop rather than at Ian.

"Actually, it wasn't me. I had gone home for a short visit with my family—yes, that's where you followed me—and one of the other agents arrested him while I was out of pocket."

Aurora's head snapped up. "What? What did you say?" She shivered. Her temples pounded like a migraine was coming on.

"Really?" Sarah draped herself across half the table, getting close to Ian's face, like she wasn't sure she heard what she heard and wanted to touch him to confirm his statement. "So, we're safe? You've got the culprit in custody?" She sighed. "I can't believe it. That's great news. Can you give us any of the details?"

Aurora couldn't get much of a breath. Her chest felt weighted down like her heart was full of rocks. She shook all over.

Ian reached out. "Are you okay, Aurora? I thought you two would be elated at this news since you'd made it your business to investigate on your own."

She reached down inside herself for a gulp of deep-lung air. She pushed Ian's hand away. "Give me a minute. This is just so much to take in." Ian and Sarah had no idea.

Sarah said, in a business-like voice, "You all have been able to tie him to the dead women who've been found in this area?"

"The woman who escaped helped a lot once she had a good night's rest and remembered more details. In case you're wondering, he does own a white pickup truck."

"You've found evidence that confirms he's the killer?" Aurora asked, still feeling like she couldn't breathe.

"Right. He's in custody. I returned as soon as I heard and was able to take part in the interrogation. His truck has been completely dismantled in a search for any material that would tie him to the women. A judge issued a search warrant for his premises. The search turned up the trophies he kept." Ian drained the dregs of his coffee, squeezed the cardboard cup into a ball, and tossed it into the trashcan.

"Did he confess?" Aurora worked hard to keep her voice from breaking.

"No, but we don't need a confession. There's plenty of evidence. Anyway, I just wanted to let the two of you know so you could sleep better at night. We'll be able to get a conviction with no problem."

"Well, Ian, you know that woman who lived across the street from Aurora's house? Did y'all find out for sure what she was doing here? I read in her obit that she worked for a detective agency. Was she trying to find that guy? Is that why she was here?"

"Yes. The parents of a victim from a little while ago in Houston proper had hired her to try to find the killer." He pushed out his chair and rose. "I'll walk you ladies to your car. I'm sure your guests are wondering what happened to you."

Sarah said, "I texted Taylor to let her know where we are and what we'd be doing."

Ian chuckled. "Of course you did." He opened the coffee shop door for them.

Before they parted ways on the sidewalk, Aurora said, "Thanks for letting us know. I guess the blood on the knife in my barn came back to her, the woman across the street? That means that man—who you believe to be the serial killer—was on my property, right? And probably what I heard that night, the scream that I thought could have been in my head, from a dream, was real. If that was the case, the killer was the person behind the light in the barn."

"Right. We haven't been able to tie the knife and blood and her death to him, yet, but I suspect we will soon. The investigation is only in the beginning stages."

Aurora bent her head back and peered up at Ian who was backlit by the sun. She held her hand over her eyes like a visor and studied him. She could say a lot of things in response to what he'd informed them of today, but what she did say, though she hadn't meant to even though she'd been thinking it, was, "What I'm wondering is, if the man y'all have arrested was the person in my barn, why didn't he kill me, too?"

"Who knows, but I assure you, you're safe now."

"I feel sure you're right about that. I *am* safe now."

Acknowledgments

The author wishes to thank the following early readers/critiquers:

Galveston Novel and Short Story Writers: Saralyn Richard, Ginny Fite, and Phyllis Moore

Cypress group: Steve Malone and Regina Olson

AND Susan Reyna: You know how helpful you've been!

THANK YOU FOR READING!

If you enjoyed *THE LIGHT IN THE BARN,* I would appreciate it if you would help others to enjoy this book, too.

Share it with a friend.

Recommend it. Please help others find this book by recommending it to friends, readers' groups, and discussion boards.

Please tell other readers why you liked this book by reviewing it wherever you purchased your copy. If you do write a review, please send me an email at **susan@susanbaker.com** so I can thank you with a personal email.

If you'd like to receive news of events and publications, please go to https://www.susanpbaker.com

To check out and/or order Susan's other books, please visit:
http://www.books.by/judge-susans-bookstore

BOOKS BY SUSAN P. BAKER

friend for murder while fighting gender and racial prejudice in a small Texas town.

Ledbetter Street

A Novel of Second Chances: Not just the story of a mother fighting for custody of her disabled son, but one of love, tragedy, and the relationships of the women of Ledbetter Street.

Suggestion of Death

An investigative reporter who can't pay his child support searches for the killer of deadbeat dads, before he becomes the next victim.

UNAWARE

Attorney Dena Armstrong wants to break out from the control of the two men dominating her life, unaware that a stranger has other plans for her.

Texas Style Justice

Judge Victoria Van Fleet aspires to the highest court in the land, but is she willing to pay the price?

The Light in the Barn, A Domestic Thriller

Is the person behind the mysterious light in Aurora's barn the serial killer who is victimizing women in her neighborhood?

NONFICTION:

Heart of Divorce

Divorce advice especially for those who are considering representing themselves.

Murdered Judges of the 20th Century

True stories of judges killed in America.

Fly Catching

An eclectic collection of short pieces.

www.susanpbaker.com

www.ingramcontent.com/pod-product-compliance
Lightning Source LLC
Chambersburg PA
CBHW051509260626
47162CB00008B/2886